TRIPLE TROUBLE PLUS ONE

BOOK 3

SLEEPAWAY CAMP
THE HOFFMAN'S BEST SUMMER EVER!

by
Diane C. Wander

Printed in the United States of America

First Printing, 2018

ISBN: 978-0-9970558-5-6 (paperback)
ISBN: 978-0-9970558-6-3 (hardcover)

This novel is a work of fiction. Where some of the characters are based in part on the personalities of real people, the names and incidents are fictitious. Where the settings are based on real places, the incidents that take place at these settings are the product of the author's imagination and are used fictitiously.

Dedication

This book is dedicated to a very special group of people who had extraordinary influence on the lives of this author and her four children.

Thank you to:
Paddy and Adele Feldman
and
Nat and Ann Greenfield
past and present owners and directors of Camp Robindel
in Center Harbor, New Hampshire

∽

Thank you to:
The Sobel Family
Doc, Puff, John, and Bart
past and present owners and directors of Camp Winaukee
in Center Harbor, New Hampshire

∽

At Camp Robindel for Girls and Camp Winaukee for Boys, my children and I learned so many important values, including friendship, sportsmanship, teamwork, respect, loyalty, cooperation, and independence. Thank you, Robindel and Winaukee. This is my love story to you!

TABLE OF CONTENTS

I.

CAMPS MINEOLA AND ADIWANDO HERE WE COME!

Eleven-year-old Brayden Hoffman could not wait any longer. He had to get out of bed. Although it was still dark out, Brayden was too excited to sleep. This was the day he had been dreaming about for months. Today, he was going to sleepaway camp.

But Brayden wasn't the only one in his family who 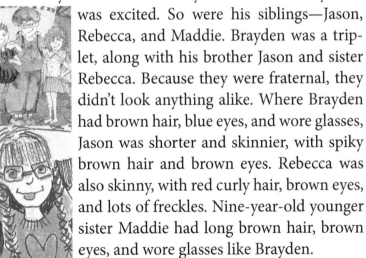 was excited. So were his siblings—Jason, Rebecca, and Maddie. Brayden was a triplet, along with his brother Jason and sister Rebecca. Because they were fraternal, they didn't look anything alike. Where Brayden had brown hair, blue eyes, and wore glasses, Jason was shorter and skinnier, with spiky brown hair and brown eyes. Rebecca was also skinny, with red curly hair, brown eyes, and lots of freckles. Nine-year-old younger sister Maddie had long brown hair, brown eyes, and wore glasses like Brayden.

Grabbing for his glasses, Brayden ran out of his room into the upstairs hallway.

"Jason, Rebecca, Maddie," he shouted. "Get up!"

"Chill, Brayden!" Maddie said, as she opened her bedroom door. "Rebecca and I have been up a long time."

"Me too, bro," Jason shouted from inside his bedroom. "I'm already dressed."

The Hoffman foursome couldn't wait to get to Camp Mineola for Girls and Camp Adiwando for Boys on Lake Winnipesaukee in the White Mountains of New Hampshire. Although they had to wear camp uniforms every day (blue shorts and white t-shirts with camp logos for the girls, and blue shorts and yellow camp t-shirts with logos for the boys), they didn't care. They all loved camp because there was so much to do. There were all kinds of team sports, such as basketball, soccer, baseball and football for the boys, and softball for the girls. Individual sports included tennis, golf, and archery, and more! At the waterfront, campers could swim, sail, and waterski. Where all the campers had arts & crafts and theatre, the girls also enjoyed gymnastics and dance. If you liked adventure, ziplining was the best. Campers could climb a 26-foot-high wall, put on a protective harness, and then zipline down a steel wire to the bottom. Nothing could be more thrilling than that!

Jason left his bedroom and headed for the bathroom, where he put gobs of gel in his hair. When he was satisfied that his hair was perfectly spiked, he poured the rest into five small plastic bottles. Jason knew that you weren't allowed to take more than 3 ounces of any kind of liquid on a plane. Gel was something he could not live without all summer long.

"What are you doing?" Brayden asked, as he entered the bathroom. "Are you bringing that junk to camp? Nobody cares what your dumb hair looks like."

"Better than looking like a slob," Jason growled.

Brayden ignored Jason's comment. Following him out of the bathroom into his bedroom, Brayden closed the door.

"So where is it?" Brayden whispered.

"Where's what?" Jason asked.

"You know what I'm talking about."

"You mean this?" Jason said, as he pulled a huge Ziploc bag filled with all kinds of candy bars from under his bed.

"Yeah! When did you get all that?" Brayden asked. "I don't have half that much!"

"Can't tell you that, bro," Jason said with a big smile. He then wrapped his candy in his windbreaker jacket and stuffed it into the bottom of his bag.

Brayden went back to his room to get dressed and pack his stash of candy. Meanwhile, Rebecca was sitting on the floor in her bedroom where she had dumped all the stuff from her backpack. With her door closed so no one would bother her, she searched for a good place to hide her mini pink glitter make-up bag filled with eyeshadow, blush, and lip gloss. Clutching it to her chest, all she could think about was making sure her mother didn't find it. She thought Rebecca was way too young to wear make-up.

Ridiculous! Rebecca thought to herself. *Where can I hide it?* Rebecca's eyes moved back and forth over all the stuff on the floor. *I know! My high-top Converse sneakers. She'll never see it there.*

Rebecca quickly put her make-up bag in her sneakers, wrapped them in her sweatshirt, and pushed them to the bottom of her bag. After throwing in all the rest of her stuff, she zipped it up and ran downstairs.

"I'm ready!" she shouted. Rebecca flopped down on the family room couch next to Maddie.

"Hey!" shouted Maddie. "Move over. You're sitting on my bag."

"Why should I?" Rebecca said. "Put your dumb backpack on the floor."

Maddie pulled her bag from under Rebecca's leg and placed it gently by her feet. Inside were her two favorite possessions. She had the USAG team leotard she'd earned when she made the gymnastics team this past spring and her *American Girl* doll, which never left her bed no matter where she slept.

Maddie was just about to grab for the TV remote when Mom and Dad came into the family room.

"Time to go, girls," Mrs. Hoffman said.

"What about breakfast?" Rebecca asked.

"No time for that. Bagels, juice, and water are already in the car."

"Let's go, boys!" Dr. Hoffman shouted up the stairs. "We don't want to be late!"

Brayden and Jason came storming down the stairs. The foursome ran out the door and piled into the van, not caring where they sat. It didn't even bother them that they had to squeeze together to make room for their bulging bags.

The only thing that mattered was getting to the airport on time.

Arriving at Fort Lauderdale Hollywood International Airport, the first challenge was finding a parking space in the garage. After driving up a number of ramps, they reached the top floor.

"There's one!" Brayden shouted. "Park the car, and let's get outta here."

As they piled out of the car, Mrs. Hoffman looked at her children. They were so excited.

"You kids are so lucky!" Mrs. Hoffman said, sighing. "I wish I were going back to camp." *That was the best time in my life,* she thought to herself.

"Your mother is right, "Dr. Hoffman added. "What could be better than a summer in the Northeast away from the heat and humidity of Florida?"

But the Hoffman foursome was not listening. They had already started walking ahead of their parents. Entering the airport, their first stop was the Jet Blue ticket counter so that Mom and Dad could get special passes to accompany their children to the departure gate. Next was Security.

"Look at the line!" Brayden shouted. "This is worse than Disney World!"

Hundreds of passengers were slowly moving through a maze of long, winding lines. This was summer time, and everyone seemed to be going on vacation. Twenty long minutes later, the Hoffmans reached the security checkpoint. Jason and Brayden immediately dumped their backpacks on the conveyor belt.

The girls took their time, and it made Brayden furious.

"Move it, girls!"

"Chill, Brayden," Jason said. "We're almost there."

"This is just so dumb!"

"Enough!" Mrs. Hoffman said. "This is not a joke. Security is important."

Rebecca and Maddie were now behind Brayden.

"What stinks?" exclaimed Maddie, holding her nose and looking around.

"It's Brayden!" Rebecca yelled. "His feet…they're gross!"

Mom turned around to look down at Brayden's feet. He was wearing unwashed white socks that were stained with dirt and sweat.

"Why are you wearing dirty socks?" Mrs. Hoffman asked.

Trying to avoid his mother's question, Brayden looked away.

"What happened to all your clean socks?" Mrs. Hoffman persisted.

Brayden turned slowly back around to face his mother. "I think I packed them all in my duffle you already sent to camp," he mumbled.

"Three dozen pairs? Why?"

Brayden shrugged his shoulders. He really had no idea why he had packed all his socks in his duffle.

"Let's just get through security, and then we'll throw these away."

Brayden nodded. Within minutes, the Hoffmans were done with the checkpoint and on the way to their departure gate.

"Race you to the gate," Jason shouted to Brayden.

"You're on!"

As the boys took off down the concourse, the girls walked slowly with Mom and Dad. Gate #58 was not that far away. Although they couldn't wait to see their friends, they wanted to be with their parents a little longer before they had to say goodbye.

When the girls arrived at the gate, Brayden and Jason spotted their sisters.

"Over here!" Jason yelled. "You gotta check in with Counselors Jeff and Anna."

Camps always sent counselor escorts to make sure the kids got there safely. Jeff worked at Adiwando and Anna, at Mineola.

"Hi, girls. Welcome back," said Anna. "It's great to see you."

As Anna gave the girls a quick hug, their friend Jana Miller came running over to them.

"Rebecca! Maddie! Come sit with Leslie and me."

Jana was Rebecca's best friend, and her younger sister Leslie was Maddie's. Although the Miller sisters were two years apart, they looked a lot alike. They both were tall and thin and had long black hair pulled back into ponytails.

7

Rebecca and Maddie followed their friends to their seats. Just as they sat down and began to talk, their flight was announced.

"Good morning, passengers. This is the pre-boarding announcement for Jet Blue 10:00 AM flight #1070 to Boston. We are now inviting passengers with small children, passengers requiring special assistance, and campers to begin boarding. Please have your boarding pass and identification ready."

Brayden and Jason jumped up and grabbed their bags. Before they could escape, Dr. Hoffman caught them from behind.

"Not so fast!" ordered Dr. Hoffman.

"How about saying goodbye?" Mrs. Hoffman said. "We're going to miss you so much!"

Turning around, the boys gave their parents a quick hug and kiss and ran to the head of the boarding line.

"Hang on, kids!" shouted Jeff. "No camper is boarding yet!"

"Why not? We want to be first on the plane," Brayden said.

"No, Brayden. You first need boarding passes," Jeff replied. "Get in line in front of Anna."

"Ugh!" the kids moaned as they raced to be first.

"No pushing!" Jeff snapped. "The plane's not leaving without us."

Meanwhile, Maddie and Rebecca were standing with their parents waiting to the very last minute. Dr. and Mrs. Hoffman put their arms around their girls for final hugs and kisses.

"Seven weeks is such a long time," Mrs. Hoffman said sadly.

"Don't worry, Mom," Rebecca responded. "Visiting Day is just a few weeks away."

"We gotta go, Rebecca!" Maddie said.

"Bye, Mom! Bye, Dad!" the girls shouted, as they ran off to join their friends. As they reached the line for boarding passes, Rebecca saw her eight-year-old "camp sister," Lexie, clinging to her mother. This was Lexie's first summer at sleepaway camp.

Since the Camp Mineola directors knew how hard it could be for a new camper, every girl in Junior camp had one or two camp sisters to help them throughout the summer. During the winter, Rebecca had received a letter from camp telling her all about Lexie. She knew it was her job to make Lexie feel welcome. Rebecca had called her a few times during the school year and had even met Lexie and her mom at the mall. But now Lexie had to say goodbye to her mom and dad. Rebecca remembered how scared she'd felt that first summer.

"It's gonna be okay, Lexie," Rebecca whispered. "It feels kinda scary now, but I promise you'll love camp. I'm going to make sure you have a great time. We're sisters now!"

Lexie wiped her tears with the sleeve of her sweatshirt and hugged Rebecca. With a big smile, she gave her parents one last kiss, grabbed Rebecca's hand, and got on line. It wasn't long before they got to the front.

"Rebecca and Lexie!" Anna exclaimed. "I put the two of you together—Row 30, Seats A and B."

"Cool!" shouted Lexie, as she pulled Rebecca's hand. "Let's go. I can't wait to get to camp!"

The girls boarded the plane and found their seats. During their three-hour plane trip to Boston, the campers kept themselves busy running back and forth among their seats, singing camp songs, and stuffing themselves with Jet Blue's free soda and sweets.

When the plane finally landed, brothers and sisters said goodbye to one another and boarded separate buses to each of their camps. Two hours later, each bus reached its camp's own colorful wooden arches. As the girls passed through Camp Mineola's gate, they could be heard shouting out each letter of their camp's name over and over again.

"M – I – N – E – O – L – A!   M – I – N – E – O – L – A!"

And on the other side of the lake, the loud voices of the boys echoed back,

"ADIWANDO! ADIWANDO! GO, ADIWANDO!

The summer camp season had officially begun!

2.

WELCOME TO HUMMINGBIRD HAMLET

Eager to get settled, the Florida girls collected their gear and raced off the bus. As they pounded along the dirt paths to their cabins, clouds of dust could be seen rising in the air above them. When the dust cleared, the most beautiful view greeted their eyes. Lake Winnipesaukee looked like a sheet of glass and sparkled as the sun spread its shining rays.

"It's so beautiful here!" Rebecca shouted. "Smell the air, Jana!"

Nothing smelled better than the hemlock and knotty pine trees that surrounded Camp Mineola.

"Later, Rebecca. Let's go!" Jana said impatiently.

Pulling Rebecca by the arm, the girls set off again on the path towards Intermediate Camp. It had been ten months since they had last seen their friends, and Jana couldn't wait.

"Hummingbird Hamlet!" Jana yelled. "We're here!"

Hummingbird Hamlet was the name of their bunk. It got its name because of all the tiny hummingbirds that made hum-ming sounds as they flapped their wings in

11

the back of their cabin. Campers loved to stand by their windows and watch the birds buzzing around the feeders. Rebecca and Jana climbed the cabin stairs and entered the screened-in porch. Just as they walked in, three of their bunkmates came running out to greet them.

"Rebecca! Jana!" Emily shouted.

"What took so long?" Sarah asked. "We've been here for hours!"

"Come on, guys. We live in Florida," said Jana.

"Well, you're here now. That's all that matters," said Chloe.

Emily and Sarah were from New York and were identical twins. With long black hair and hazel eyes, they looked exactly alike except that Emily had a beauty mark on her right cheek. Chloe came from Massachusetts. Like Rebecca, she had red curly hair and freckles.

As Rebecca and Jana entered the cabin, the biggest smiles flashed across their faces.

"OMG!" Rebecca shouted. "Stacy Starshine! Are you our counselor?"

Stacy was one of the most popular counselors at camp and everybody's favorite waterski instructor. She also had the most amazing blue eyes, which sparkled like the stars in the sky above Lake Winnipesaukee. Ever since she came to Camp Mineola, she had been known as *Stacy Starshine*.

"I can't believe we get you this summer," Jana exclaimed.

"And I'm so glad you're here," Stacy said, as she hugged Rebecca and Jana.

"Who are our other counselors?" Jana asked.

"Us!" answered Jenny and Randy, as they walked into the cabin with tennis rackets in hand.

"Meet Jenny and Randy," Stacy said. "Guess what they'll be teaching this summer?"

"Tennis!" all the girls shouted.

"Cool!" Jana said. "I always choose tennis as an elective."

Electives were activities that campers got to choose on their own. In Intermediate Camp, the girls had two of them every day.

"Well, now that you girls have met all of us, I think our group should have a special name," Stacy said. "Any ideas?"

"I know!" Counselor Jenny blurted out. "Since there are ten of you and three of us, let's call our cabin *The Lucky Thirteen!*"

Stacy, Randy, and all the girls burst into laughter and cheered. The campers in Hummingbird Hamlet could not believe their good fortune—three fabulous counselors and ten best friends forever. The girls couldn't wait to share the good news with their parents. Knowing that they needed a letter home to get into the Dining Hall, they all got busy writing.

As the sun set on Lake Winnipesaukee, the ten girls walked arm in arm to dinner. With letters in hand, they entered the Dining Hall where everyone was cheering. Camp was off to a great start!

Rebecca

Dear Mom and Dad,

We're here! I'm in Hummingbird Hamlet with all my friends. And guess what? Stacy Starshine is one of our counselors. I can't wait to go waterskiing on Stacy's boat. She is the best! Maybe I'll get up on one ski this summer!

I know you want us to write longer letters, but I just got here and have to go to dinner. Bye!

Love,
Rebecca

3

A Not So Welcomed Welcome to Buttercup Burrow

"From East to West, our camp is best!
From state to state, our camp is great!
From lake to lake, we take the cake!
Go Mineola!"

"I can't believe we're finally here!" Leslie shouted.

"Me neither," Maddie yelled back.

As the two best friends sat down at their table in the Dining Hall, they began to cheer along with their bunkmates. This summer, there were twelve of them in their Junior Camp cabin called Buttercup Burrow. Named because of all the buttercups growing in the grass on the side of the cabin, the campers always loved to pick them. They would put a buttercup under their chins to see if the flower's shiny petals made a yellow reflection. If it did, that meant you liked butter. They all secretly hoped that their chins would shine. This would give them a good excuse for spreading lots of butter on the yummy fresh baked dinner rolls every evening.

15

And on this very first evening, Maddie and Leslie were seated at the end of their cabin's table, where a big basket of piping hot dinner rolls had been placed. Sitting next to them were two new campers—Blair from California and Abby from Texas. Where Blair had long blond hair, blue eyes, and was very thin, Abby had wavy short brown hair, brown eyes, and was chubby.

In between bites of dinner rolls with melted butter, the girls cheered and sang camp songs. Abby tried to join in, although she didn't know the words. Blair, however, sat quietly with her arms crossed tightly on her chest. She had a big frown on her face, with her lips tightened and turned down at the ends.

"That cheer is so lame!" Blair whined. "Do you do this at every meal?"

"Yeah!" Maddie snapped, with a look of disgust on her face.

"Not to worry, Blair," said Leslie, trying to make her feel better. Leslie knew they were supposed to do everything they could to make new campers feel welcome.

"Once you learn the cheers, you'll be doing it, too," Leslie added.

"Will you girls teach me?" asked Abby.

"Why would anyone want to learn those dumb cheers?" Blair said, glaring at Abby and Leslie. "I hate this camp. I'm calling my parents to take me home."

None of the girls knew what to say. Maddie especially felt bad that she had snapped at Blair.

"It's okay, Blair," Maddie said. "Everyone gets homesick their first summer. Once you get used to camp, you'll love it!"

"What do you know?" Blair said. "This place is the worst. I'm outta here!"

Blair jumped up from the table and ran out the dining room door. With all the cheering, no one except Maddie, Leslie, and Abby seemed to notice. Knowing that campers were never allowed to leave the dining room alone, Maddie jumped up from her seat. She ran to the front of the dining room where Katie, their counselor and Junior Camp Unit Head, was monitoring the salad bar.

"Katie!" Maddie exclaimed. "Blair is gone. It's not our fault! We were trying to be nice to her, but she acted so mean. She said she hates camp and thinks our cheers are dumb. She wants to go home."

Katie took out her walkie talkie and sent an alert to all counselors and staff.

"She couldn't have gone far. I'm sure we'll find her. Thanks for telling me, Maddie."

Wiping tears from her eyes, Maddie went back to her seat. All her bunkmates crowded around her.

"What happened, Maddie?"

"Blair told Leslie and me she hates camp. We tried to make her feel better, but she just got madder and ran out. It's getting dark, and she doesn't know her way around."

"I don't want anything bad to happen to her, but she should go home!" Gabby said, frowning.

Gabby was a camper from New York. She always made sure everyone knew what she was thinking.

"No one's going home!" shouted Laci and Rory, Buttercup Burrow's two other counselors.

"I'm surprised at you girls," chided Laci.

"Yeah, sit back down," said Rory. "We need to talk."

By this time, all the campers in other cabins had finished dessert and were filing out of the dining room.

"What about our cupcakes?" Gabby asked.

"Cupcakes will have to wait," Laci snapped. "You know how hard it can be coming to camp for the first time. Don't you remember how all of you felt last summer? You were homesick, too. The only difference between you and Blair is that you girls had each other. Blair feels left out."

"But Abby isn't homesick, and she's new," Leslie said. "She even tried to do the cheers with us."

"Everybody reacts to camp in their own way," Rory answered. "Besides, Abby came to camp with her big sister, who is in Senior Camp. All of you who have sisters here know how good that feels when you're sad or homesick. Blair came alone and all the way from California. You need to be more understanding of how she feels."

"But when Leslie and I tried to be nice to her, she was just mean," said Maddie.

"I don't think Blair was trying to be mean," said Rory. "Right now, Blair feels all alone. Without her parents and friends who are far away, she probably is frustrated because she doesn't know what to do to get rid of the scary feelings inside her. Some people cry when they feel like this. Others get angry and lash out at others. I think that's why Blair was mean to you."

"Maybe that's why I yelled at Gabby last summer," Maddie responded. "On our first night, I was homesick. Gabby picked up my American Girl doll. I thought she was gonna take it. That scared me. My doll goes everywhere with me. She makes me feel safe."

"That's right, Maddie!" said Rory. "*Safe* is the key word. Right now, Blair doesn't feel safe. The big question is what each of us can do to make her feel that way."

"While we're figuring all this out, maybe some yummy chocolate and vanilla cupcakes will help," Laci suggested.

"Yay!" the girls cheered. As they all grabbed for their favorite flavor, they started shouting out ideas. When Blair was found and came back to their cabin, there was no way she would not feel welcome. Junior Camp Buttercup Burrow's girls would make sure of it!

4.

BLAIR'S RETURN

By the time the girls got back to Buttercup Burrow, Blair was not there. Assuming she soon would be found, they quickly put together a special welcome celebration for her.

First, they put a plate of chocolate and vanilla cupcakes on her dresser. Although it wasn't Blair's birthday, each cupcake had a candle so Blair could make lots of wishes for a great summer at camp.

Next, they created a "Welcome to Buttercup Burrow" poster for her. Counselor Rori had stopped by the Arts and Crafts Shack to get poster board and colored markers. After each camper wrote a special message to Blair, they placed the poster on the entry door in their screened-in porch.

Lastly, they invited Blair's two older camp sisters, Jana from Hummingbird Hamlet in Intermediate Camp and Sophie from Sandy Flats in Senior Camp, to join their celebration. Each of them had brought a special treat for their new camp sister—chocolate kisses from Jana and the cutest little teddy bear from Sophie.

21

The girls did not have to wait long. As they finished their preparations, Blair walked in with their counselor, Katie, and Camp Director Fran Goldstone.

Forgetting about the way Blair had behaved in the dining room, Maddie and Leslie ran right up to her.

"Blair, are you okay?" Leslie said. "We're so glad you're here."

"I'm sorry if I made you mad," Maddie added. "Look! We all made a special poster for you."

Blair turned around and looked at the poster. As she read each message, tears welled up in her eyes. As much as she wanted to respond to Maddie, Leslie, and all the girls, the lump in her throat was too big. Jana and Sophie, her camp sisters, stepped in to comfort her.

"You don't need to say anything, Blair. The first day of camp is scary," Jana said, hugging her. "I brought you some chocolate kisses."

"I got you a gift, too," Sophie added. "A Camp Mineola teddy bear!" Handing her the cuddly stuffed animal, Sophie proclaimed, "You are now officially one of us!"

For the first time, a slight smile appeared on Blair's face. As she looked around at her bunkmates, her counselors, and camp sisters, all the anger, fear, and sadness that had been tied up in a knot inside her body seemed to disappear.

"Thank you," Blair whispered. "I'm sorry I was so mean."

"That's all over now," Katie said, as she put her arm around Blair. "You're safe, and we'll all be here for you."

"We still have one more important thing to do," said Lacy. Walking Blair over to her dresser, Lacy continued.

"The girls didn't want you to miss out on dessert, so they brought back cupcakes for you."

"We even got candles!" Maddie said. "You gotta blow out each one."

"And make lots of wishes for the best summer ever!" shouted Leslie.

After Blair blew out the candles, Camp Director Fran had the biggest smile on her face.

"I'm so proud of all you girls," she exclaimed. "On your very first night, you have shown what it means to be a good friend. You have also shown *empathy*. Do any of you know what *empathy* means?"

All the girls looked at each other to see if any of them knew the answer, but no one responded. When Fran started to answer, Blair shouted out.

"I know! That was one of my vocabulary words this year. I think it means sharing someone else's feelings. Just like today when all the girls felt sad because I felt sad."

"That's right, Blair!" Fran answered. "And from *empathy*, we get the word *empathetic*. You girls in Buttercup Burrow are *empathetic*. Quite an accomplishment for the first night of camp!"

As Director Fran hugged all the girls and said good night, Rory and Laci broke into a new cheer:

"Buttercup Burrow is the Best.
Number One of all the rest.
The best of friends we'll always be
because we have empathy!"

Maddie

Dear Mom and Dad,

Camp is great! I'm with all my friends from last summer. A new girl named Blair ran away from camp during dinner because she was homesick. That was scary! When they found her, we made her a welcome party. That made her feel better.

I can't write anymore now. Laci and Rory need to collect our letters. Lights are already out. Gotta go.

Love,
Maddie

5.

ADIWANDO ARRIVAL

Just like Rebecca and Maddie, Brayden and Jason were so excited when they arrived at Camp Adiwando. Where the girls couldn't wait to get to their cabins, the boys ran off the bus and made a beeline for the basketball court.

"Look who's here!" yelled Matthew. "The Florida gang!"

"It's about time you arrived!" Aaron shouted. "Get over here so me, Matthew, Ethan, and Conner can beat the pants off you! Florida boys vs. kids from the Northeast."

Matthew and Ethan were from New York. Aaron was from New Jersey, and Conner was from Connecticut. The four of them had been in the same bunk with all the Florida boys for the past three summers.

"You're on!" shouted Brayden, Jason, Jake, and Dylan.

"But you guys from the Northeast are no match for us boys from the South," Jason bragged. "The first team to reach 11 wins."

Just as they were getting into their game, an announcement came over the loudspeaker.

"Welcome, Adiwando Mainland campers! Now that you're all settled into your cabins, it's time to get our summer off to a great start. Everyone to the Dining Hall and then onto the bonfire!"

Cheers erupted from the hordes of campers who piled out of their bunks on Junior and Senior Row. But the Florida boys and Northeast gang ignored the call to dinner.

"No way we're stopping now," Brayden shouted. "We're up by 4 points!"

"We can't be late," Matthew responded. "We'll get in trouble."

"You're just saying that cuz you're losing," said Jason. "Besides, we're the oldest kids now on Senior Row. We can do anything we want!"

"I don't think so, Hoffman," chided Counselor Jordan. "You Florida boys are late! Dump your stuff in Cabin 28 and get to the Dining Hall. Looks like all you guys might miss out on dessert. Get movin' now!"

Jordan was one of Cabin 28's counselors, along with Jeff, who escorted the Florida kids to camp. All the kids loved Jordan but knew better than to disobey his orders.

"No way I'm missing dessert the first night of camp," Brayden yelled, as they ran to their cabin. "They always have ice cream sundaes. My mouth is watering just thinking about them!" The boys dumped their bags on their bunkbed. Where they would usually argue about who gets the top bunk, they had no time. Dinner and dessert were their only thoughts as they flew out the door.

❧

Thirty minutes later, dinner was over. Although they had to eat fast, the Cabin 28 boys managed to stuff themselves with lots of pizza and ice cream sundaes. As everyone left the Dining Hall, the sun was setting over Lake Winnipesaukee. Campers old and new couldn't believe how beautiful the sun looked, turning from yellow to gold and then to orange as it sunk in the western sky. Even more spectacular were the roaring flames of Adiwando's first bonfire of the summer.

The campers rushed to the wooden benches that encircled the campfire site and burst into a cheer.

"Adiwando is the best!
Better than all the rest.
We always have lots of fun
because we are Number 1!
Go Adiwando!"

When the cheering died down, Camp Director, Bud Savin, put up his hand to get everyone's attention. Buddy, as he was known to all campers and counselors, began to speak.

"Welcome, Adiwando campers! We are so happy to have all our old campers back for another summer and our new ones who are here for the first time. We begin our summer like we always do, with a big bonfire next to our *Tree of Values*. Our old campers know that our tree has six branches. These stand for *Cooperation, Loyalty, Friendship, Sportsmanship, Achievement,* and *Enthusiasm.* Because these values are so important, I want all our new campers to come forward and stand by me."

As the new boys joined Buddy, not a sound could be heard except for the wind making tiny ripples on the lake. All the old campers knew that the ceremony that was about to take place was very special and required absolute silence. They could not wait for Buddy's next words.

"I am now going to give each one of you a golden leaf with one of our six values written on it. When I call your name, shout out your value, and drop your leaf into this big burlap bag. When you are done, I will empty all the leaves into our bonfire. While our six important values burn brightly, they will be reminders to all of us to work hard all summer long to cooperate, be loyal, be a good friend, show sportsmanship, achieve, and be enthusiastic."

One by one, the boys called out each value over and over again. And when the last camper was done, the burlap bag was overturned, and the leaves were thrown into the fire. As the flames crackled and got bigger, the campers broke into a cheer once again.

"ADIWANDO! ADIWANDO! GO, ADIWANDO!"

Buddy then put up his hand to signal silence.

"Before we conclude, we have one more tradition. Will the boys in Cabins 25-28 come forward."

The Senior Row boys got up quietly and walked solemnly to where Buddy was standing.

"As our oldest groups on the Mainland, you will now receive the golden branch from our *Tree of Values*. It is your responsibility to be role models for all our younger campers. If you want to graduate to our Island camp next summer, you need to prove yourself worthy. Are you up to the job?" he shouted.

"Yes!" the boys responded in unison.

The oldest campers then passed the golden branch from one to the other until it reached Cabin 28 counselors Jordan and Jeff. With the golden branch in both their hands, campers got up group by group and left the bonfire. As the flames crackled and began to die out, they all walked quietly back to their cabins to get ready for bed.

At 9:00 PM, lights went out and talking stopped. Taps—the bugle call ending the day—resounded throughout the camp. When Taps was over, campers wanted to stay up and talk with their friends, but exhaustion got the better of them. After a long day of traveling and their evening bonfire, all they could think about was sleep. The bugle for Reveille—morning wake-up time—was just a few hours away.

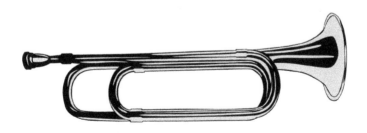

6.

Day 1 at Camp Adiwando

The sounding of the bugle at Reveille was never wel-comed by any camper except on the first full day of the camp season. When the blaring noise echoed from cabin to cabin, Adiwando campers jumped out of their beds and rushed to get ready. Within minutes, they were dressed in their blue and yellow camp uniforms with teeth brushed and hair combed.

"Let's go, boys!" Jordan said. "Time for breakfast."

"And make sure you bring your letters to the Dining Hall," Jeff added. "No letter, no candy."

All campers were required to write home three times weekly. Although they didn't like this task, most felt that a piece of candy for a letter was a fair trade.

When they got to breakfast, Jeff was standing by the door.

"Here, Jeff," Jason said, as he grabbed the letter in Brayden's hand. "Brayden and I decided to write one letter from the both of us. No reason we should bore our parents with the same stuff twice."

"Besides, one letter will save on stamps," Brayden added.

"Good thinking, bro!"

"No…not good thinking, Jason," said Jeff. "There are no special rules for twins or triplets. One letter per camper. Right after breakfast, both of you will be writing your own letters, and I'll be checking them."

"But that's the time we get to pick all our electives for the week," Brayden whined. Campers had three assigned activities every day and two of their own choice.

"Well, I guess you and Jason will be picking last this week," Jeff responded. "Unless you consider letter writing one of your electives!" As Jeff laughed, the boys walked into the Dining Hall.

"It's not fair," Brayden said. "I already wrote a letter from the both of us. Why should I have to do it again?"

"Stop whining!" Jason snapped. "Eat your breakfast so we can get back to the bunk."

The boys scarfed down pancakes and maple syrup and raced back to the cabin.

"I still don't want to write another letter," Brayden muttered.

Just write a couple lines and sign it. That's what everyone does."

"But Mom and Dad get mad when we don't write enough," Brayden replied.

"It's only the first day!" Jason said. "What could you have to write about? Just scribble something, and let's get outta here. I hope it's not too late to pick basketball and football as my electives this week."

"Okay! Okay!" Brayden said as he threw Jason a pen. "We gotta hurry. I want sailing and basketball."

The boys finished their letters quickly, got them okayed by Jeff, and ran out the door. Reaching the sign-up board, they saw Jake and Dylan, their Florida pals, nearing the front of the line.

"Hurry up, Hoffmans! We saved you a place!"

"Thanks, guys," Jason said, as he patted the boys on their backs.

Within minutes, all of them had chosen their electives and had gotten their top two choices. Week 1 at Camp Adiwando was off to a good start!

Brayden

Dear Mom and Dad,

Camp is great! I'm in Bunk 28. We had a great bonfire last night. I can't write much cuz I'm late to pick my electives for the week. The bugle is blowing. Gotta go....

Love,
Brayden

Jason

Dear Mom and Dad,

I don't have time to write a letter, but my counselor is making me. He wouldn't let Brandon and me write one letter together. I think that's dumb. TTYL! My fans are waiting for me.

Love,
Jason

7.

THE CAMP MINEOLA BIG SURPRISE

Back at Camp Mineola, the first week seemed to fly by. From wake-up at Reveille, the girls' schedules were packed full. Breakfast, clean-up, and three morning activities were followed by lunch, rest hour, and three afternoon activities. By the time dinner and the evening program were over, the campers welcomed their return to their cabins.

And when they were getting ready for bed, there were two events that occupied the thoughts and conversations of all campers. The first was the upcoming visit of Adiwando boys who had sisters at Mineola. Every Sunday, campers who had brothers or sisters at Adiwando and Mineola got to see one another for an hour during Rest Hour.

The second was *Blue and White Color War*, which also took place on Sundays. The girls in each cabin were divided into the blue and white teams and competed in all kinds of sports. Color War always began sometime in the beginning of the summer with an amazing surprise *breakout*. None of the campers knew when Color War would start, but when it did, the breakout was spectacular! The girls couldn't wait, but they knew that the wait was always worth it. And this summer's Color War breakout was about to top them all!

&

"Hurry up, Maddie! Finish your burger already. The boys will be here soon," Rebecca said impatiently.

Sunday lunch was always a cookout—the favorite meal for most campers. What could be better than juicy hamburgers with gobs of ketchup, hotdogs with mustard, sour pickles, potato chips, and your choice of soda? Nothing was going to get in the way of Maddie finishing the best meal of the week.

"Chill, Rebecca! I'm not leaving till I get my chocolate chip cookie. Besides, I want to get some for the boys. Brayden and Jason love Chef Billy's cookies. Can you believe he was baking them when Mom was here as a kid? He must be so old!"

"I love them, too," Rebecca said, "but you're gonna have to wait. There's some kind of meeting we all have to go to now…even the boys."

"That's weird! Who told you that?" Maddie asked.

"My counselor, Stacy, but she promised that we'd get the cookies at the meeting."

As the girls began walking towards the camp entrance to meet Jason and Brayden, two Adiwando buses came through the gate.

"Attention Mineola girls! Please report to the Dining Hall for a very special welcome meeting to greet Adiwando campers. Whether you have a brother or not, all Mineola girls are invited."

Coming off the bus, Jason and Brayden shouted to their sisters.

"Hey, why are we going to a meeting?"

"We don't know what's going on," Rebecca answered. "But if you want one of Chef Billy's cookies, that's where you gotta go."

"For chocolate chip cookies, I'll go anywhere," Brayden said, with a big smile on his face.

"Me, too," Jason said, nodding. "But before I forget, we have something for you."

Before the girls could say anything, a Kit Kat bar came flying at Rebecca and a Snickers Bar at Maddie.

"Nice catch, girls. I was sure you'd miss," Jason teased.

"Thanks!" Maddie said.

"Mmmmm!" Rebecca said. "There's nothing better than a Kit Kat bar."

"Let's go already!" Brayden shouted. "I can't wait any longer."

All the girls and boys crowded into the Dining Hall. When everyone found a seat or a spot on the floor, Mineola Camp Directors Neil and Fran Goldstone got everybody's attention. Then Neil began to speak.

"Welcome, Adiwando campers, to our first brother-sister visit of the camp season! I know you are all probably wondering why we have asked you to meet here. To help answer this question, I'd like Adiwando Director Bud Savin to come forward and join Fran and me."

As Bud walked to the front of the Dining Hall, Neil continued speaking. "At both of our camps, we stress many important values. At Mineola, sisterhood is first on the list. We want our girls to treat each other as if they were sisters."

"And at Adiwando, we stress brotherhood," Director Bud added. "We want our boys to treat each other as if they were brothers. But equally important are good brother-sister relationships. That is why our two camps have had the tradition of inviting siblings to visit their brothers or sisters for many, many years."

"Maybe as long as we have been eating Chef Billy's famous chocolate chip cookies," Director Fran exclaimed. "Bring them out, Chef Billy!"

Cheers and applause resounded throughout the Dining Hall as Chef Billy and his staff circled around with trays of warm, gooey cookies. Once all the campers had been served, Neil continued.

"Now I know all of you are eager to get outside, but before we end our meeting, we have one very special thing to do. How many of you know the story of how our two camps got their names?"

Not a sound could be heard throughout the Dining Hall. As campers looked around at their friends, blank faces stared back at them.

"Well, I guess it's about time you know this story!" Bud shouted. This won't take long, and we think you'll enjoy it."

The dining room got very quiet. As Director Bud was famous for his "Buddy Stories," the boys were especially eager to hear what he had to say.

"500 years ago, there was a legend about a great Indian chief named Wonaton. He lived on the north side of the lake we now call Winnipesaukee. Chief Wonaton had a beautiful daughter named Mineola, who he always protected from danger."

"On the south side of the lake lived an enemy Indian tribe. The chief of this tribe, named Adiwando, was very young. He had heard stories about Chief Wonaton's beautiful daughter and wanted to meet her. One day, when Wonaton was away from his village, Adiwando came to meet Mineola. The two young people fell in love. When Chief Wonaton found out, he became very angry and began chasing Adiwando with his tomahawk. Mineola begged her father not to kill him and convinced him to let her marry him."

"On the day of the wedding, all the people got into their canoes. It was a tradition for wedding ceremonies to take place on the lake. But on this day, the sky was dark and gray. Although bad weather was expected, a miracle happened. When the canoes reached the middle of the lake, the sun came out, and the water began to sparkle. But this 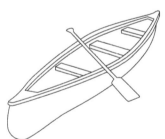 only happened around the canoes of Mineola and Adiwando. Chief Wonaton thought this was a very special sign and proclaimed that these waters would be called "Winnipesaukee." This is the Indian name for the "Smile of the Great Spirit" that shined down upon the two lovers."

"So, Lake Winnipesaukee got its name. And many years later, our camps became known as Mineola and Adiwando as symbols of the bonds of love and friendship that tie us together."

With the legend finished, Neil stepped up to the microphone. "And now that you know the story about how we got our names, we'd like you to meet Mineola and Adiwando's great-great-great-grandchildren, who have traveled from their home on the other side of Lake Winnipesaukee to share a surprise with you."

Suddenly, the campers heard drum rolls that got louder and louder. Then, they heard the sounds of pounding feet coming nearer. Within seconds, the back door of the dining room flew open and a young man and young woman dressed in Native American clothing ran through the Dining Hall chanting and beating their drums. When they got to the front of the room, Directors Neil and Fran raised their arms and demanded silence. Fran then spoke to their guests.

"Welcome to Camp Mineola. We thank you for coming here at our request. What message do you have for our campers?"

The young man spoke.

"My name is Adi. I am the great-great-great-grandson of Adiwando and Mineola. This is my sister, Minea, their great-great-great-granddaughter. Long, long ago, our families had many tribal wars. The tomahawk killed lots of  people. Thanks to our great-great-great-grandparents, Adiwando and Mineola, the tomahawk has come to symbolize values such as friendship, teamwork, love, and respect. So that is why we are here today, to hand over to you this very special tomahawk."

As the tomahawk was passed to Fran and Neil, they looked at its message, lifted it high in the air, and shouted,

"Blue and White Color War Starting Now!"

And with Fran and Neil's words, the campers began to cheer, stamp their feet, and pound on the tables. As blue and white confetti streamed from hidden bags in the ceiling, they screamed louder. When the directors were able to finally get all the campers to settle down, Neil spoke.

"I want to thank Adiwando Director Bud and all his campers for being a part of our Color War breakout. We are so happy you were all here with us today. Now it's time to say goodbye. Mineola sisters look forward to seeing their brothers next week, when they visit you at Adiwando."

And with Director Neil's last words, the boys left Mineola. Although these campers did not get to spend much time with their sisters, they did not complain. They had just seen the coolest Color War breakout ever. What could top that?

8.

BASEBALL BLUNDER

Ten minutes later, the boys were back at camp just as Rest Hour was ending. As Brayden and Jason got off the bus, all their friends were running out of their cabin to get to their activities. Just like Mineola, Sundays were special days at Adiwando, but not because of Color War. At Adiwando, Color War took place at the end of the summer for five days. Sundays were special because it was time for Tribal War!

Campers were divided into four teams with Indian names and competed all day long. At the end of the day, everyone got together for the weekly Indian Tribal Council and bonfire. Dressed in Native American attire, staff members gave out *Tree of Value* awards to deserving campers. Although campers loved to win the tribal games, they liked winning a *Tree of Value* award even more. They understood that the best kind of winning is when you got rewarded for upholding Adiwando's six important values: *Cooperation, Loyalty, Friendship, Sportsmanship, Achievement,* and *Enthusiasm.*

43

Adiwando boys looked forward to Tribal War all week long. So, when Rest Hour was over, they couldn't wait for the games to begin.

"Hoffmans, let's go!" their bunkmates shouted. "Tribal War is starting now."

Brayden was a "Nashua," and Jason was an "Ossipee." These were names of tribes that lived in New Hampshire long, long ago. Although the brothers were on different teams, they never got angry with each other when one lost and the other won. Jason and Brayden never let a game come between them. Their friendship always came first.

The two brothers ran into their cabin and got their mitts. Within minutes, they were at the baseball diamond with their teammates. When Bunk 28's counselor Jordan blew the whistle, the Nashua and Ossipee Teams from Cabins 25-28 were ready to play. Brayden's team—the Nashuas—was up at bat first, and Jason's Ossipees were in the field.

"Okay, boys," Jordan said. "This is a six-inning game. The team with the most runs at the end of six wins. I know you all want your team to win, but let's remember that we are here to have fun. Put in your best effort and focus. It doesn't really matter what  the scoreboard says at the end of the game. Remember that campers who show teamwork, sportsmanship, and try their best are always the winners. Now let's play ball!"

The Nashua's first batter was Jake.

"Okay, Florida boy! Show them what you got!" his teammates cheered.

But Jake wasn't sure he had what it would take to get on base. His pal Dylan was on the pitching mound, and he had the camp's record for the most strike-outs.

"Strike One!" Jordan shouted.

Jake swung again.

"Strike Two!"

"Let's go, Jake. You can do it!" the Nashuas screamed.

"Strike Three, Jake. You're out."

"That's alright! That's okay! We can beat 'em anyway!" cheered his teammates.

Next up was Oliver Wells from Bunk 26. He was a new camper from London, England and had never played baseball before. But that didn't concern his teammates. Oliver had told them that he was a soccer and field hockey player on his school team back home in London. So, when Oliver got up to bat, all the kids were sure he'd get on base.

But Oliver was nervous. This was the first time he had ever swung a bat. He wished he hadn't told his bunkmates that he played sports at home. From the eager looks on the faces of his teammates, he knew he had made a big mistake. Dylan was known for his fast ball, and that's what Oliver got on the first pitch.

"Strike One!" shouted Jordan.

"Come on, Oliver. Show us your stuff!" his team cheered.

What stuff? he thought to himself, as Dylan's curve ball came across the plate.

"Strike Two!"

Oliver had one more chance. He had to get on base. He choked up on the bat the way Jake had done. When the ball came across the plate, Oliver swung as hard as he could and hit the ball all the way to left field. He stood there in shock!

"Run, Oliver!" Brayden shouted.

Oliver dropped the bat and began to run. He knew he was a fast runner, so getting on base would be easy.

"Hey, where are you going?" Jake yelled.

"Wrong way!" the team shouted. "First base, not third base!"

All the boys started to laugh. They could not believe what they were seeing. Oliver stopped dead in his tracks. His face turned all colors of red. As tears started to well up in his eyes, Jason, who was playing first base on the opposing team, ran over to him.

"That hit was amazing, Oliver!" Nobody on our teams socks a ball like that. Taking him by the arm, Jason led him to first base. "Put your foot right here. If the next ball is hit, run to second. The Nashuas are lucky to have you!"

The laughter stopped immediately. Both teams began to cheer, "Ollie! Ollie! Ollie!" Oliver, with his new nickname, breathed a sigh of relief. Jason had come to the rescue, and now Ollie knew what he had to do. With a big smile on his face, he looked towards second base with hopes that he would get a chance to run there when his next teammate came up to bat.

Brayden came to the plate. Knowing how to deal with Dylan's pitches, he swung and hit a double. As Brayden began running, Oliver ran from first to second, to third, and Home. His wish had come true! Not only did he get to run to second base, but he scored a run for his team! Nashuas and Ossipees alike cheered for both Oliver and Brayden. Even though the Nashuas scored, it was okay. It just felt good to cheer no matter what team the boys were on.

The game ended after six innings, with the Ossipees winning 3-1. As good as the Nashuas played during most of the game, Dylan struck out batter after batter.

"Amazing game, boys!" Jordan said. "You guys really showed teamwork and sportsmanship. I am especially proud of you, Jason. You showed Oliver what our Adiwando brotherhood is all about."

And that night at the Tribal Council, Jordan wasn't the only one who was proud of Jason. When the Sportsmanship award was announced, Jason Hoffman was called up to hang the wooden plaque with his name on the *Tree of Values*. Although Brayden secretly wished he was getting an award, too, he could not help but cheer for his brother, who really deserved this award. Both Hoffman brothers could not think of a better way to end Tribal War Sunday.

Jason

Dear Mom and Dad,

Today was awesome! We had tribal war games. A kid from London ran the bases the wrong way in our baseball game. When everyone started to laugh, I went over to him and showed him the right way. Everyone stopped laughing and cheered. I got the sportsmanship award at the Tribal Council. Don't tell anyone I said this, but I think this award is better than all my basketball and baseball best player trophies put together!

Love,
Jason

Brayden

Dear Mom and Dad,

We went to see the girls today. We had so much fun. Our camp was part of their Color War break-out. It was really cool! The best part is that we got Chef Billy's chocolate chip cookies. They are so good. Maybe you'll get them when you see the girls on Visiting Day! If you do, bring us some when you visit us.

Love,
Brayden

9.

S·U·C·C·E·S·S!!!

Monday morning, the girls at Camp Mineola were back to their usual routine. Although they wished that Color War competition had started right after "break out," they knew they had to wait until the next Sunday for the games to begin. And when Sunday came, Maddie and Rebecca would be playing for the White Team. Their best friends, Jana and Leslie, were on the Blue Team. Although they were disappointed that they were not all on the same team, Color War was only one day a week.

Besides, the girls loved all their activities the rest of the week. There were so many fun things to do. Maddie's favorite was gymnastics. Although Junior Camp girls only got one elective activity, Maddie had special permission to go to gymnastics for two periods every day. This was because she was on the USAG Gymnastics Team and needed to train all summer long. Maddie didn't mind missing out on other activities. Gymnastics was everything to her. From the minute she got up in the morning, all she could think about was practicing her routines on the beam, uneven parallel bars, vault, and mats.

Rebecca wasn't into gymnastics. Her favorite activities were waterskiing and Arts and Crafts. Since she was in Intermediate Camp, she got to pick two electives every day. So, whenever these activities were available, Rebecca could be found waterskiing or in the Art Barn doing all kinds of art projects, such as: ceramics, painting, drawing, or even making jewelry, stained glass, or candles.

When the bugle for third activity blew, Rebecca ran to the ski shack. She wanted to be first in line at the boat dock.

"Wait, Rebecca!" Jana shouted. "I'm coming, too."

Rebecca slowed down. "Hurry up. If we get there early, we'll be on the first boat. I gotta get up on one ski!"

"You're already on one ski," Jana said. "I saw you drop a ski last week and ski for a few seconds without falling."

"Yeah, but now I need to start on one ski and stay up. That's so much harder."

"If I can do it, you can, too," Jana said. "You've got to be positive! Besides, Stacy Starshine will be there to help you."

"Did I just hear my name?" Stacy asked, as the girls arrived at the ski shack. Without waiting for an answer, Stacy continued. "Jana is right, Rebecca. I will be there coaching you. Today is the day, and you're going up on one ski and staying up!"

"If you say so," Rebecca responded in a hesitant voice.

"I know so! Now hop on the boat. Let's go skiing!"

Rebecca, Jana, and the next three girls in line got on the boat. When it stopped in deep water, Rebecca jumped in, and Stacy threw her a ski.

"Okay, Rebecca, put both your feet in the binders of the ski."

"They're in," Rebecca yelled.

"Good! Now pull your knees up to your chest and crouch up as much as possible. Pretend you're a ball. Are you ready?"

"I think so."

"All right! When the boat starts to move, let the boat pull you. Don't fight it. Count to about five, and then when the ski doesn't feel wobbly, stand up. Got it?"

"Yes!" Rebecca shouted. "Go!"

Evan, the other ski instructor, hit the gas.

"1-2-3-4-5…." Rebecca counted aloud. "I'm up! I'm up!"

Stacy gave her a thumbs-up and had the biggest smile on her face. Rebecca couldn't believe she had gotten up on one ski. Although she could not hear above the noise of the motorboat and the waves, she could see the other skiers on the boat cheering for her. All she needed to do was stay up.

Don't fall! Don't fall! Rebecca said to herself. *You can do it!*

Before she knew it, she had completed one full rotation. When Stacy gave her the hand signal, she let go of the rope. Everyone on the boat could hear her yelling, "I did it! I did it!"

The boat circled around to pick up Rebecca.

"I'm so proud of you!" Stacy said. As she helped Rebecca into the boat and unbuckle her life preserver, all the girls came over to give her a hug.

"Nice going, Rebecca!" Evan said, as he gave her a high-five. "One more run like that, and you'll be ready to cross the wakes on one ski."

Rebecca beamed. Now she knew she had done well. A high-five from Evan was very rare. All the girls were shocked, even Stacy. While the rest of the campers skied, Rebecca closed her eyes and replayed her turn over and over again in her mind. She just couldn't believe she had actually gotten up on one ski and that she would soon crisscross the waves.

When all the skiers had their turns, the boat returned to the dock just in time for the bugle ending third activity. Rebecca and Jana jumped off the boat and went to their cabin to change for lunch. As they reached Hummingbird Hamlet, Maddie came running by.

"Maddie!" Rebecca yelled. "I did it! I got up on one ski and didn't fall!"

Maddie stopped in her tracks. "Wow! That's great, Rebecca. And guess what? Goldie said that my beam routine today was my best."

Goldie was Camp Mineola's gymnastics coach. She had once been an alternate gymnast on the USAG Olympics team.

"Goldie said if she were a judge, it would be a *Perfect 10!* Can you believe that?"

"Go, Maddie!" Jana shouted.

"Go, Hoffman girls!" Rebecca and Maddie said at the same time.

The three girls burst into laughter and high-fived one another.

Although Rebecca and Maddie did not love to write letters home, today they couldn't wait to tell Mom and Dad their very good news.

Rebecca

Dear Mom and Dad,

I did it! I got up one ski and stayed up! I am so happy and can't wait to show you when you come on Visiting Day. Only two weeks away. I can't wait!

Love,
Rebecca

Maddie

Dear Mom and Dad,

Today was the best day ever! Maybe better than the day I made the USAG team. Coach Goldie said my beam routine was a Perfect 10. She would know because she was once on the Olympics Team. Maybe one day it will be me!

Love,
Maddie

10.

PARENT INVASION!

The first four weeks of camp flew by. When Parent Visitation was just days away, campers could not believe that more than half the summer was now over. Although this special day was a reminder that they would be returning home three weeks later, campers did not waste any time feeling sad because they could not wait to see their parents. And their parents could not wait to see them.

As much as it was exhausting to be a mom and dad to triplets plus one more, Dr. and Mrs. Hoffman missed their fearless foursome all summer long. It was just too quiet at home. They looked forward to their two full days of visitation—one for the boys and one for the girls.

The first one took place at Camp Mineola, where Rebecca and Maddie eagerly awaited their arrival Friday morning after Bunk Clean-up. When the bugle for first activity came blaring into the cabin, all the girls in Hummingbird Hamlet ran out of the bunk.

"Forget first activity. Let's go meet our parents," Jana shouted to Rebecca.

"We can't do that, Jana."

"Why not?" asked Maddie, as she and best friend Leslie caught up to the girls. "Nobody gets in trouble for not following the rules on Parent Visitation Day."

Although it was hard to admit it, Rebecca knew Maddie was right. Besides, she wanted to see Mom and Dad as much as her sister did.

"Let's go," said Rebecca. "Let's get to the gate before our counselors catch us!"

As they began to run towards the camp entrance, many more Mineola girls had the same idea. Although they all privately feared getting in trouble for not going to their first activity, nothing was going to stop them from meeting their parents at the front gate.

Lucky for the girls, they didn't have to go that far. Before they got halfway to the camp entrance, hordes of smiling parents came walking down the path laden with bags and bags of goodies. Screams of excitement echoed throughout the camp. It was hard to tell who was shouting louder, the campers or the parents.

"Rebecca! Maddie!" Dr. Hoffman shouted.

The girls ran faster, right into their parents' arms.

"I missed you so much!" Rebecca said.

"We missed you, too!" Mrs. Hoffman exclaimed, "and we have lots of goodies for both of you."

"Thanks, Mom," Maddie responded. "But we need to get to first activity. I have gymnastics. You have to see my beam routine. It's getting better and better all the time!"

"Then you're coming to my second activity," Rebecca said. "You gotta see me waterski!"

"But first we need to get rid of these bags," Mom said.

"My cabin's right here," Rebecca responded. "Let's dump them all on my bed, and then we'll meet Maddie and Dad at gymnastics."

"Don't you need to go to your first activity?" asked Mom.

"Not really. When there is more than one kid in a family, they let us go wherever we want just as long as we stay with our parents. So, I'm going to Maddie's first activity, and she's coming to my second."

"Let's go, Dad!" Maddie shouted, as she pulled his hand.

"Not to worry, Maddie girl! Have your mother or I ever missed one of your routines?"

"No," Maddie answered. "But there's always a first time, and it's not going to be today!"

For the next two hours, Dr and Mrs. Hoffman's cell phone cameras were in action. First, they watched Maddie repeat her "Perfect 10" beam routine. And then they got to see Rebecca start on one ski and even go over the wakes. They were so proud of their girls!

After a fabulous buffet lunch with lots of Chef Billy's chocolate chip cookies for dessert, the girls brought their parents back to their cabins. They couldn't wait to go through Mom and Dad's goody bags. Like every summer, the bags filled to the brim did not disappoint. In addition to new hair accessories for Maddie and a mini artist's drawing and painting set for Rebecca, there were Kit Kat Bars, Snickers, chocolate nonpareils with rainbow sprinkles, Pringles, Doritos chips, and salsa. Best of all were Dr. Hoffman's homemade sweets. This year it was chocolate chip brownies, enough for all the girls in Rebecca and Maddie's cabins.

"Thank you, so-o-o much!" Rebecca shrieked.

"I can't believe how much stuff you brought us," Maddie added.

"Just don't eat it all at once," Mrs. Hoffman warned. "We don't want you to get sick."

"Don't worry, Mom. We'll be okay. Our counselors won't let us eat too much," Maddie said, with a big smile on her face.

Dr. and Mrs. Hoffman did not know why Maddie was grinning so much. They just thought she was happy to have so much good stuff. But Rebecca knew. As the two sisters exchanged looks, they realized that Mom and Dad were not aware that counselors were going to dump all the uneaten sweets after one day. Before the bugs invaded and everything spoiled, the girls would have a 24-hour food fest. This was information they chose not to tell Mom and Dad.

At the end of afternoon activities, it was time for parents to leave. Although the girls were sad to see their parents go, they loved sleepaway camp and knew that they'd be going home in a few weeks. As they began to walk toward the exit, Rebecca stopped in front of her cabin.

"Wait, Mom and Dad. I have something I want you to give the boys."

Rebecca ran into her bunk and came out with a bag.

"What's in the bag, Rebecca?" Mom asked.

"Chef Billy's cookies! You know how much the boys love them. While we were eating lunch, Maddie and I collected a bunch for them. Bring them to the boys tomorrow."

"And make sure they know it's from us!" Maddie added.

"Do I get to eat one?" asked Dad.

"Just one," Rebecca answered. "And only because you made us those yummy brownies."

Dr. and Mrs. Hoffman laughed, as did Rebecca and Maddie. After hugs and kisses, the girls said goodbye and returned eagerly to their cabins to begin their 24-hour feast.

11.

Parent Invasion!
(Day 2)

Saturday morning, Dr. and Mrs. Hoffman were up early for their day at Camp Adiwando. Once again, they packed up their car with bags of treats; this time for Brayden and Jason.

Upon arrival at Camp Adiwando, they joined the crowd of parents walking through the camp's wooden arches. When they reached the center of camp, it did not surprise them that Brayden and Jason were the only boys waiting to greet the arriving parents.

"Mom, Dad!" Jason and Brayden shouted.

As the Hoffmans hugged their sons, Dr. Hoffman asked, "Are you the official welcome party for all parents?"

"No! But we finished our clean-up early and were given special permission to wait here for you and the other parents. After all, we're the oldest campers on the Mainland," Jason bragged.

"Yes, indeed! You are the oldest campers," Counselor Jeff said, interrupting. "And should know better than to think your parents are going to believe that story. Welcome to Adiwando, Dr. and Mrs. Hoffman. Nice to see you again. But your sons need to get back to our cabin to finish clean-up. Your parents will be out here waiting for you, boys."

"Come on, Jeff," Brayden whined. "We already made our beds."

"But you didn't sweep, and Jason didn't empty the garbage—your jobs this week. Did you forget?"

"Okay, okay," Jason said. "But we need to first take those heavy bags off our parent's hands."

"No!" Mrs. Hoffman said sternly. "Clean-up first."

Fifteen minutes later, Jeff and Jordan welcomed the Hoffmans as well as the other campers' parents into a now spotless Cabin 18. Happy to rid themselves of their heavy bags, parents dumped all the food and sweets on their kids' beds.

"Look at all this stuff!" Brayden shouted.

Like Rebecca and Maddie, Jason and Brayden got all kinds of candy bars, Twizzlers, Gummy bears, nonpareils, chips, and salsa.

"Thanks, Mom and Dad," Jason said. "You're the best!"

"There's more!" Mom exclaimed. "Dad made brownies for your entire bunk, and your sisters sent you a bag of Chef Billy's chocolate chip cookies."

"This is better than three trips to Jaxson's for ice cream!" Brayden shouted.

Jaxson's was the Hoffman kid's favorite ice cream parlor back home in Florida. Brayden loved the triple scoop ice cream cones.

"Okay, boys," Jordan interrupted. "Time for first activity. Out to the baseball field for a parent-camper baseball game. Bunk 28 versus Bunk 27."

"Let's go," Jason shouted. "Bunk 28 can't be beat—especially with us four Hoffmans on the team."

"Wait! What about Dad's brownies?" Brayden asked, as he stuffed one in his mouth.

"Later, bro. Our team awaits!"

Six innings later, the bugle blew to end first activity. Just as Jason predicted, Bunk 28 beat 27 by five runs thanks to the Hoffman family. Both Jason and Brayden hit homers for their team. Amazingly, so did Dr. Hoffman. And Mrs. Hoffman got to second on a high fly to centerfield. The boys couldn't believe how well their parents played.

"You made us proud today, Mom and Dad," said Jason. "I was sure you'd both strike out. Thanks for living up to the Hoffman name."

Dr. and Mrs. Hoffman couldn't help but laugh. Neither could Brayden. As Jason was the family comedian, they never knew what to expect next. For the rest of the day, the boys played basketball, soccer, and went swimming while their parents took videos from the sidelines. At the end of the day, Brayden and Jason walked their parents to Camp Adiwando's wooden arch. After a quick hug and kiss goodbye, the boys ran back to their cabin.

When the boys left, Dr. and Mrs. Hoffman looked at each other and smiled. Although camp visiting days were exhausting, they loved the time they had just spent with their kids. As they watched their sons and daughters playing sports and interacting with their friends and counselors over the past two days, they knew that there was no place better for their fearless foursome than a summer at sleepaway camp.

12.

MOUNT WASHINGTON ADVENTURE

With Parent Visitation over, Adiwando campers looked forward to Trip Day. Four times each summer, the boys went on camp adventures, such as sporting games, water parks, beaches, and sailing trips. For the boys in Bunks 25-28, this Trip Day was the one they looked forward to all summer long because they were going to hike up Mount Washington—the tallest peak in the New England states. Since this hike was difficult, it was only offered to the oldest campers on the Mainland. Jason, Brayden, and all their friends couldn't believe that they were finally old enough to go!

When Trip Day arrived, the boys were awakened long before Reveille to get ready for their major hike. They dressed quickly in their climbing attire—nylon zip-off pants, Camp Adiwando t-shirt, windbreaker jacket, wool socks, hiking boots, and baseball cap. The boys then checked to make sure their backpacks had all their provisions. When it got cold or rained, they needed extra short and long sleeve shirts, a fleece jacket, an extra pair of wool socks, and even a winter cap. Their backpacks also contained Chapstick, sunglasses, an emergency blanket, a flashlight, energy bars, fruit, and a refillable water bottle. In addition to these supplies, their counselors would be carrying first aid kits just in case…. This was going to be a serious day of hiking!

Once they were ready, the boys boarded their buses. After a two-hour trip, they arrived at the base of Mount Washington. It was 7:00 AM; the sun was shining; and the mountain peak could be seen in the far distance.

"Everyone off the bus," Jordan ordered. "Breakfast first, bathroom break, and then Mount Washington here we come!"

All the boys began to cheer. Grabbing their backpacks, they got off the bus and assembled by a picnic area, where breakfast boxes filled with bagels and cream cheese, a banana, raisins, and orange juice were distributed. Eager to begin their hike, the boys ate quickly.

The boys were then organized into groups of four, with one counselor and a Mount Washington guide.

"Florida boys!" Jeff shouted. "Brayden, Jason, Jake and Dylan, you're with me in Group 1 with Evan as our guide. Now listen up so you know what to do and what *not* to do."

The boys moved in closer to listen to Jeff and Evan.

"Okay, Group 1," said Evan. "We're going to start our hike by the Cog Railway tracks unless…." Evan paused. "Do any of you want to take the easy way up the mountain? It's only three miles riding on the Cog Railway, but five miles if you hike to the top. At the top, there will be bathrooms, a cafeteria, and a gift shop. But we have a long, hard climb before we get there."

The boys looked from one to the other. The Cog Railway looked really cool with its different color cars and caboose. *It certainly would be easier,* they thought to themselves. *But how could they face all the other campers if they didn't hike?*

"No way!" the boys shouted.

"Group 1 is walking to the top!" Brayden exclaimed.

"Alright then," said Evan. "Everyone buddy up."

"Brayden, you're with Jake," Jeff said. "And Jason, you're with Dylan."

Evan continued to give directions. "We'll be taking the Jewel Trail. First, we'll cross the railway tracks and then a bridge over the river. When we hit our first mile, we'll cross Clay Brook and stop for our first buddy check and a water break. Let's go!"

The first mile was a cinch. When they got to their first stop, everyone was doing fine and eager to move on. Evan, however, was not so quick to go.

"I know you boys feel great, but you need to pace yourselves. Right now, it's no big deal, but it won't be that way as we get further along. You need to stay with your buddies and keep a slow and steady pace. The next part is a two-mile stretch. When we hit Mile 3 marker, there'll be a log bench and a small fire pit. There we'll take a longer break and refuel. Water and snacks are very important. Onward and upward!" Evan shouted.

The boys continued to walk. As the weather was sunny and warm, the group had removed their jackets and zipped off their nylon pants to make them into shorts.

"I don't know why we needed all the warm clothing in our backpacks," Brayden complained. "It's hot, and I'm sweating."

"I am, too," said Jake. "But I think the weather's gonna change the further up we go."

As the boys climbed higher, the weather did get colder. The sun was still out, but the wind picked up. By the time Group 1 reached the fire pit, all the boys had put on their windbreakers and re-zipped their pants.

The boys placed their backpacks on the ground and flopped down on the wooden bench. Evan had been right. After three miles, they were tired and needed a break. They were very glad they had stuffed their bags with protein bars and fruit. They were starving and couldn't eat their snacks fast enough.

"Slow down, boys!" Evan said. "You need to pace yourselves with eating as well as hiking. Take a break and look above and below you. What do you see?"

"So cool!" Jason exclaimed. "The Cog Railway is way down there."

"And I see Mount Washington above us," Dylan added.

"That's right, boys. We are now at the *tree line*. Do any of you know what that means?" Evan asked.

"I know!" Brayden said. "We learned about that in science this year. The *tree line* is the last place where trees can grow. Above that line, they stop growing because it's too high and too cold."

"Very good, Brayden," praised Evan. "When we finish our break, we will begin walking above the tree line. The trail will become rocky. We won't have dirt paths like the ones so far. You will need to walk carefully from rock to rock."

"It's very important that you keep to the trail," Jeff warned. "Look for the blue trail markers. There will also be *cairns* to guide you."

"What's a *cairn*?" Jake asked.

"I know!" Brayden blurted out. "It's a bunch of rocks piled together as a marker so you don't get lost on a trail."

"Good going, bro!" Jason said. "Maybe you should be our guide."

All the boys began laughing.

"Very funny, Jason," Jeff said sarcastically. "But I think we'll leave the guide work to Evan."

"Thanks, Jeff," Evan said with a smile. "We now need to get very serious. The last part of our hike is the most difficult. We have about two miles left to get to the top. That may not seem like a lot, but it will feel that way because it's so hard. The minute we leave here, it will start getting foggy. You'll feel like you're in the clouds. That's how it is above the tree line. The higher we go, the more the wind will start gusting. That will make it hard to walk. So, I want all of you to stick close to your buddies. You'll also need to change your clothing...long sleeve shirts, fleece jackets, and winter caps. Remember to refill your water bottles at the water tap, and make sure to put on lots of Chapstick. You need to keep your lips moist. Get to it, boys. We're out of here in five!" Evan commanded.

"Do you think it's gonna be as hard as Evan said?" Brayden whispered.

Jason wasn't sure but thought it was a good idea to act positive.

"We're a team!" Jason exclaimed. "Together, we can do anything! High-fives for Group 1!"

Five minutes later, they were on the trail again. Evan was in the lead with Jeff in the rear. As the six hikers moved very slowly towards the summit, the path became rockier. The wind got stronger, and the fog made it almost impossible to see the blue trail markers and cairns. As much as the boys wanted to keep in communication with their buddies, the howling wind prevented them from hearing one another. Climbing from rock to rock, each boy reached for his buddy's hand. Although they were embarrassed by the idea of holding hands, they knew they would do anything they needed to do to get safely to the top.

The boys plodded along slowly. The wind got even stronger, and the temperature dropped at least 10 degrees. Evan was further ahead with Jason and Dylan. When Brayden, Jake, and Jeff were about 100 yards from the summit, they heard Jason and Evan's echoing voices.

"We made it! We made it! We're at the top!"

Brayden and Jake shouted back, but the wind would not allow their voices to be heard. Suddenly, rain began pelting down on them. The rocks got very slippery.

"We're almost there," Jake yelled to Brayden. Holding onto each other as tight as possible, they climbed at a snail's pace.

"One more step," Brayden shouted, and......

"THUMP!"

Brayden and Jake turned around. Jeff had fallen.

"Keep going, boys," Jeff shouted. "Go to the top and send Evan. I twisted my ankle on a rock."

The boys looked at each other. As much as they wanted to be at the top, there was no way they were going to leave a member of their team alone.

"Jake, go get Evan," Brandon yelled. "I'll wait with Jeff."

Dropping his backpack, Brayden slowly inched down the incline to where Jeff was lying across the rocks. Looking at Jeff's eyes, Brayden could tell that he was in a lot of pain.

"Don't worry, Jeff. We're gonna get you out of here! Evan will be here soon."

Brayden picked up Jeff's bag and then looked at him.

"Do you have anything in here for pain? My parents always give us Advil."

"Yeah," Jeff said in a weak voice. "In the First Aid kit next to my bag."

Brayden opened the kit quickly and gave him two Advil and his water bottle.

"There's something else you gotta do. I learned a special word in Health class that helps you when you get injured.

What was that word?" Brayden said aloud as he hit his hand on his forehead…. "I know! *RICE!*"

"What do I need rice for?" asked Jeff.

"Not rice to eat. *RICE* stands for *Rest, Ice, Compression,* and *Elevation.* You have to reduce the swelling by resting your ankle, putting ice on it, wrapping it snugly, and keeping your leg propped up."

"How do you remember all that?" Jeff asked.

"My mom and dad say I have a really good memory."

"Thanks, Doc," Jeff said with a smile.

Although the rain was still coming down and the wind was blowing hard, Brayden wasn't scared. He knew help was on its way. Within minutes, Evan and two mountain rangers came slowly down the incline. When they reached Jeff, they unrolled a stretcher and lifted him onto it.

"You okay, Brayden?" Evan asked.

"Yeah, I'm fine."

Brayden and Evan walked behind as Jeff was taken to the First Aid station on the summit. When Brayden finally got to the top, he got his chance to scream. "I made it! I can't believe I made it."

Jason, Jake, Dylan, and all the other Bunks 25-28 groups were there to cheer him on. "Brayden! Brayden! Brayden!" they yelled. No one deserved a welcome to the summit of Mount Washington more than Brayden Hoffman.

All together on the summit, all the campers posed for a group picture despite the very bad weather. They then ran into the cafeteria to change out of their wet clothes and warm up.

After lunch in the cafeteria and lots of hot cocoa with whipped cream and marshmallows, the campers bought *I climbed Mount Washington* t-shirts and then prepared for their hike back to the base of the mountain.

"How will Jeff get down?" Brayden asked.

"Actually, none of us will be hiking down," Evan answered. "The weather has gotten worse. We can't even take the Cog Railway. Everyone will be taking the shuttle bus. It only takes about 30 minutes. We need to get to the base so Jeff can see a doctor as soon as possible."

Although the campers would have preferred to hike down, they were not disappointed. Exhausted from their four-hour trip to the summit, they were just as happy to take the bus—especially if it meant they could be with Jeff. Teams were meant to stick together, and that's just what the Adiwando campers and counselors were going to do!

Three hours later, the campers were back at camp in time for dinner. Wearing their new Mt. Washington t-shirts, they ran off the bus and stormed the Dining Hall. Although they were starving, the boys couldn't wait to brag to all the other campers about their mountain hike. Moving from table to table, they shared their adventures until Camp Director Buddy called for everyone's attention. The boys in Senior Row found their seats quickly.

"Welcome back, campers! I know you all had a great day on all your trips outside of camp. I want to especially welcome back our Senior Row hikers who made it all the way to the top of Mount Washington!"

Cheers and applause erupted as all the boys in Bunks 25-28 stood up and raised their hands with the "V" sign for Victory. When the campers settled down, Buddy continued to speak.

"Today's hike was a very difficult one. The boys had to deal with much colder, wetter, and windier weather than usual this time of year. Because of the wind and rain, the rocks were very slippery. Unfortunately, Bunk 28 Counselor Jeff slipped and sprained his ankle a short way from the top. Jeff will be fine, but if it wasn't for the quick thinking of Group 1 team member Brayden Hoffman, Jeff would not have gotten to safety as quickly as he did. Alone with Jeff and his buddy Jake, Brayden knew they could not leave Jeff by himself. So, he asked Jake to get help while he waited with Jeff. Even though the weather was bad and Brayden was very cold and wet, he understood that his place was with Jeff. We need to recognize Brayden for his bravery. Brayden Hoffman, please come forward and stand by me!"

Cheers erupted once again with all the campers standing and chanting, "Brayden! Brayden! Brayden!" When Brayden joined Buddy, everyone could see that his face had turned red. He just couldn't believe he was getting all this attention.

'Brayden, Camp Adiwando is very proud of you! What you did today is what we celebrate on our *Tree of Values*. Today you showed the true spirit of friendship and especially loyalty. Making a choice to stick by Jeff no matter how uncomfortable it was for you is what loyalty is all about. Today is not Sunday—the day we usually give out our weekly *Tree of Value* awards. But we are going to make an exception. Brayden Hoffman, we are giving you the Loyalty award. Your name will be added to our tree tonight and will remain there for this week and next. Congratulations!"

As Buddy shook his hand, all the counselors and campers starting cheering again. Brayden returned to his seat red-faced but smiling from ear to ear. It had been an amazing day for campers on Senior Row, but nothing compared to how Brayden Hoffman would always remember his Mount Washington adventure!

Brayden

Dear Mom and Dad,

Today we climbed Mount Washington all the way to the top. It was so cool except for the bad weather. It was really cold, windy, and rainy. Jeff slipped and sprained his ankle. I stayed with him in the pouring rain until Evan and two mountain rangers came to get him with a stretcher. When we got back to camp, Buddy gave me a special Tree of Values award for being loyal. Everyone cheered for me. Best day ever!

Love,
Brayden

Jason

Dear Mom and Dad,

Amazing day! Jason and Brayden Hoffman are now members of the "We made it to the top of Mount Washington Club." So cool! The best part is that Brayden got the Loyalty award for his bravery. First me with my award for Sportsmanship and now Brayden.

Congrats, Mom and Dad! The Hoffman boys are doing you proud!

Love,
Jason

13.

MINEOLA COLOR WAR FINALE

"I can't believe we only have one week left until the summer is over," Rebecca complained. "Soon we'll be home and back in school!"

"Why are you talking about school?" Jana asked. "Just think about camp stuff like Color War, the Sing, the banquet, and the campfire. The last week is the best of the whole summer!"

"I know," Rebecca said. "I'm just not ready to go home. Camp is my favorite place. I wish we could go to Mineola for ten months and school for two."

"Keep dreaming, Rebecca." Jana laughed. "But not now. We gotta get to practice. We only have a couple days left before the Sing. I don't know about the White Team, but the Blue Team has the most amazing songs. You're not gonna believe how good they are!"

"No way they're better than ours!" Rebecca said. "Just you wait. The White Team is ahead in Color War, and we're gonna win Sing, too!"

Rebecca ran out of the cabin but then stopped. Thinking about what she had said to Jana, she turned around and shouted, "Whoever wins, there's one thing that won't change…."

"BFF's! Best Friends Forever," the girls shouted in unison. With smiles on their faces, they each ran off in different directions to practice their Color War Songs.

Sing was a big deal at Camp Mineola. From the minute Color War broke out the first week of the summer, each team got to work on developing a story called a theme. The themes were *top secret*. Only the counselors on each team and the girls in the oldest bunks in Senior Camp knew what they were. It wasn't until Sing practice began that the themes were made known to all the campers on a team. Even then, campers had to make a promise to keep their theme "hush hush" until Sing. To make the "final reveal" more exciting, each team had a code name.

This summer, the Blue Team called themselves the "Blue Bolts" because their secret theme was about the characters in the *Cars* movies. Just like Lightning McQueen—the famous race car in these movies—they secretly hoped their team would have lightning speed. The White Team chose *Toy Story* as their theme and became known as the "White Buzz." Their hope was that all their White team girls would be superheroes just like Buzz Lightyear in this movie.

At Sing, each team would tell their story in song using three different tunes. In addition, the campers learned a fight song called a "March" and an "Alma Mater," which was a song that was all about Camp Mineola.

At Sing rehearsal, the girls practiced their songs over and over again. Each team knew it had to deliver a perfect performance if it was going to win the Sing. The campers also knew that they only had one more chance to participate in Color War games. Right now, the White Team was ahead, but anything could happen.

When Sunday arrived, the girls were psyched for their final competition. Dressed in their team colors with faces and lips painted in blue or white, the campers were ready for their last battle of the summer. As each cabin started their first activity games, team cheers could be heard echoing throughout the camp.

"Blue Bolts always lead
Cuz we got lightning speed"

"White Team Girls Got the Buzz.
We can win like no one does!"

Where Rebecca and her bunkmates in Hummingbird Hamlet were assigned to tennis, Maddie's cabin was at the volleyball court. The Blue Team had just dropped the ball, so it was now the White Team's turn to serve.

"Side out and rotate! Our team is really great!"

As the White Team cheered, positions were switched, and Maddie served the ball. Scoring 5 points for her team, her teammates applauded when they finally lost the ball to Blue.

"That's alright! That's okay! We can beat them anyway!"

But the White Team did not beat the Blue. Although they scored a lot of points in the beginning of the game, White ended up losing by two points, 25 to 23.

"2-4-6-8! Who do we appreciate?
White! White! Go, White!"

"1-3-5-9! Who do we think is mighty fine?
Blue! Blue! Go, Blue!"

Games always ended with each team cheering the other. Sportsmanship was very important at Camp Mineola.

Back at the tennis courts, White Team girls Rebecca and Emily were playing doubles against Jana and Sarah. To make sure that all the girls in the bunk got a chance to play, two girls had played singles, and two groups played doubles. The team winning the most games at the end of the activity was declared the winner. The score was now tied—three games for Blue and three games for White.

"Come on, Rebecca," Emily whispered. "We gotta beat Jana and Sarah. They won the first game, and we got the second. Just one more to break the tie!"

"I know," Rebecca said. "It's your serve, Emily. Nobody puts them across the net like you do!"

Emily whacked the ball across the net. Jana swung and missed.

"15 Love!" called the judge.

Fifteen points for us and zero for Blue, Rebecca thought to herself.

Emily served the next ball to Sarah. She swung and hit the ball into the net.

"30 Love!"

"Emily, Emily, go Emily!" the White Team girls yelled.

"Two more serves like that, and we've won," Rebecca whispered to Emily.

Emily served again to Jana. The ball went straight into the net, but Emily still had a second chance. From the look on her face, everyone could tell she was nervous.

"That's alright! That's okay! We can beat them anyway!" the White Team cheered.

A look of determination came across Emily's face. She lifted her racket, swung, and the ball went flying swiftly across the net. Jana reached for the ball but once again missed.

"40 Love!"

The White Team girls applauded. One more point, and their team would win the game. Emily served the ball to Sarah. This time she returned the ball. The two teams hit the ball back and forth until…

"WHAM!"

Jana smacked the ball hard, hoping to put Rebecca off guard.

"Out!" shouted the judge. The ball had gone out of line. "Game for the White!"

The White Team girls ran onto the court and starting hugging Emily and Rebecca. Rebecca and Emily then ran to the other side of the court to hug Jana and Sarah. Although they were on opposite teams, they were always friends first. All the girls shouted together, "Go, Blue! Go, White! Go, Hummingbird Hamlet! Go, Lucky 13!"

At the end of the day, many games had been played all over Camp Mineola, but no one knew which team had won the Blue and White competition. The campers had to wait until the Sing to hear the final scores. With this big event of the summer just two days away, there was still a lot of work to do.

14.

THE SING

For the next two days, the schedule was intense. The girls went from rehearsal to rehearsal with time off only for meals and Rest Hour. Getting ready for Sing was like practicing for Opening Night of a Broadway Show. When the evening of the big event arrived, all the girls were nervous but also very excited.

Each side of the Rec Hall had been transformed. On one end, the White Buzz had created a set that looked just like Andy's room in the *Toy Story* movies, with his toy box full of toys. On the other end, the Blue Bolts had made a raceway just like the ones in the *Cars* movies. As each team marched in, they were dressed like many of the characters in the movies upon which their themes had been based. For the White Team, you could see Lightning McQueen, Mater, Chick Hicks, Doc Hudson, and Sally, to name a few. The Blue Team's parade included Sheriff Woody, Buzz Lightyear, Sid, Andy, Mr. Potato Head, Rex, and so many more!

Once both team were seated, they each took turns singing their songs—first their marches, then their Three Tunes theme song, and finally their Alma Maters. When the Sing concluded, the counselor judges walked out to tally the scores. As both teams performed so well, no one knew who would win the Sing or the Blue and White sports competition. Everyone could feel the tension in the room while they waited for the judges to return. Twenty minutes felt like twenty hours, but finally the judges came back. Head Judge Anna took the microphone.

"Okay, Blue Bolts and White Buzz. We now have our final Color War results. Are you ready?"

The girls began to cheer, applaud, and stamp their feet. When they settled down, Anna continued.

"This summer, the score for our Blue and White sports competition is 5742 to 5740. With a difference of two points, the winner is…. the White Buzz!"

The entire White Team stood up and cheered.

"White Team Girls Got the Buzz.
We can win like no one does!"

When Anna raised her hand for silence, the girls got seated.

"And now for the Sing. Please hold your applause and cheering until I finish announcing the winners for each song and the final score. The Best March goes to…. the Blue Bolts!"

The Blue Team started to shout, but Anna raised her hand again for silence. Knowing the girls would not be able to hold back their cheering, she quickly announced the remaining results.

"The best Three Tunes Theme Song goes to the White Buzz! The best Alma Mater goes to the Blue Bolts! And now for the final scores of the Sing and Color War…."

Anna paused again. Not a peep could be heard in the Rec Hall. As the girls did not know how many points each team had gotten for each song, they had no idea who would win the Sing. They also did not know which team would win all of Color War.

"The score for this year's Sing is 151 to 149. With a difference of 2 points, the winner is…. the Blue Bolts!"

Now it was the Blue team girls time to cheer.

"Blue Bolts always lead
Cuz we got lightning speed."

Anna raised her arm one final time. "We have one final score!" she shouted.

All the campers got quiet immediately. They couldn't wait to hear which team was the big winner.

"The final score for Color War is 5891 to 5891. With a difference of zero points, Color War is a tie!"

All the campers jumped to their feet. As Blue and White Team girls ran in all directions to find their bunkmates, their shouts and cheers resounded throughout the camp. Arm in Arm, Blue Team and White Team girls walked out of the Rec Hall. What a way for Color War to end! Everybody was a winner. Nothing could be better than that!

Maddie

Dear Mom and Dad,

Color War and the Sing are over. Blue Bolts won the Sing, and White Buzz won Blue and White competition. The final score was a tie. I wish Blue had won both. Whatever...

Tomorrow is the banquet and then the bonfire on the last day. I can't wait to get back to the Harrison Street Gym. Coach Paul is gonna love my routines!

Love,
Maddie

P.S. Can't wait to see you, too!

Rebecca

Dear Mom and Dad,

Can you believe camp is almost over? Just two more days and then we leave. I wish we could stay longer! I'm going to miss all my camp friends so much. At least I have Jana. I'm so glad she lives in Florida. I also can't wait to see you.

Love,
Rebecca

P.S. Daddy, please make chocolate chip brownies. That's all the girls talk about around here. I just have to have one waiting for me when I come home. Yummy!

15.

THE TREASURE HUNT

While the girls at Mineola were recuperating from the end of Blue and White competition and the Sing, Color War was in its final days at Camp Adiwando. Although competition only lasted five days, the boys felt that Color War and Song Fest were the most exciting events of the entire summer.

Color War had broken out four days earlier when the boys had least expected it. Since there had been so many "fake" break-outs, the campers had given up thinking that Color War would ever take place. Returning to their cabins after another full day without a hint of Color War, the boys were tired and disappointed. To make things worse, a scary announcement came across the loudspeaker just as they were getting ready for bed.

"Attention counselors and campers. We have just been informed by counselors in many cabins that boys are finding bed bugs in their bunks. Counselors, please do a bed check right now, and report back to us immediately."

Shrieks and screams could be heard all over the Mainland. As the boys stripped their beds, their screams of horror turned to screams of delight. Under their blankets and top sheets, they found a "blue" or "buff" cardboard cutout in the shape of a bug announcing Color War. This time it was for real. No more fake-outs. The boys knew immediately that they were either on the Blue or Buff Team.

Brayden and Jason, being brothers, were both on the Blue Team, along with Ethan and Matthew from New York. Their Florida pals, Jake and Dylan, were on Buff, with Conner from Connecticut and Aaron from New Jersey. Although they were all totally grossed out by the thought of bed bugs, they couldn't think of a better way to break out Color War. After a restless night of sleep, competition began the very next morning.

For four days, the Blue and Buff Team boys in Cabins 25-28 competed against each other in so many sports, including baseball, football, soccer, basketball, tennis, swimming, and La Crosse. In addition, each team was getting ready for Song Fest. Somewhat like Camp Mineola's Sing, the boys had to present a cheer, fight song, and an Alma Mater.

Today was the final day of competition. This was the last chance for each team to rack up Color War points—not by playing team sports but by participating in a giant Treasure Hunt. Director Bud had just finished explaining all the rules. The boys knew that their team had to find their cabin's treasure box first to be declared the winner. As excited as the campers were for Song Fest that night, they were doubly psyched for the Treasure Hunt.

"This is the best Color War activity Buddy has ever planned," shouted Jason as they left the Dining Hall.

"I wonder what'll be in the treasure box," mused Jake.
I hope it's lots of candy, Brayden thought to himself.
"Come on, Brayden, the Blue Team needs the Hoffman

boys. Who better than us to figure out all the clues! Let's roll."

Jason and Brayden did not give Jake a chance to respond. There was no time for small talk with the Buff Team. The Blue Team boys ran out of the Dining Hall to their cabin, where counselors Jordan and Jeff were waiting to hand out the first clue. Grabbing a blue envelope for their team, Jason, Brayden, Ethan, and Matthew huddled together and tore it open. Jeff turned on the timer, and Jason read the first clue.

When you climb any mountain,
it is nice to find a fountain.

"There are so many water fountains!" Ethan moaned.

"Let's go!" Brayden yelled.

Within minutes, the boys had hit three fountains and had just arrived at number four where Matthew found their next blue envelope. Ripping it open, he shouted the clue.

An apple a day keeps the doctor away.

"The infirmary! These clues are so easy!" Brayden muttered.

They ran to the infirmary where their next blue envelope was sitting in a basket of apples. Brayden read the third clue.

Rain or shine…this place is mighty fine!

"What place is mighty fine?" Ethan asked.

"If you ask me, everything is mighty fine here," Matthew said.

"How do you *not* know the answer?" Jason asked. "It's the sports arena. You can do sports there rain or shine! Get it?"

Smiles came across Ethan and Matthew's faces. "Right!" they shouted. "Let's go!"

When they reached the sports arena, the four of them spread out to find the next clue.

"I got it!" yelled Ethan. "It's under the benches."

> *On those cold days and nights*
> *when you need a little heat,*
> *This place is so bright.*
> *It really can't be beat!*

"The Indian fire circle!" Ethan shouted. "That'll keep you warm."

"Good going, Ethan!" Jason said. "Let's go."

When they got to the Indian fire circle, they searched everywhere, but there was no blue envelope.

"Where else can you get warm?" Matthew asked.

They all stood quietly trying to come up with an answer.

"The Playhouse!" Ethan blurted out. "The big stone fireplace!"

"Go, Ethan!" they all shouted, as they made a beeline for the Playhouse. And just as Ethan said, they found lots of envelopes in a big metal container by the fireplace. Fishing through the container, they found the blue one, which said *Bunk 28 Blue Team Last Clue.*

"Just one to go!" Jason shouted. "What does it say, Brayden?"

> *Now it's time to get your treasure.*
> *Hope it gives you lots of pleasure.*
> *28…Don't waste any time.*
> *This is the end of your rhyme.*

"Huh? I don't get it," said Ethan.

"Me neither," Matthew agreed.

"Just give me a second," Jason said. Thinking aloud, he said, "None of the clues have ever mentioned our bunk number…."

"In our cabin," Brayden said. "It's in our cabin, but where? There's got to be more hints in this clue."

As the boys got to the porch of their cabin, Jason suddenly realized where the treasure was hidden.

"*Waste!* the clue said. *Don't waste any time.*"

Brayden's eyes lit up, and a big smile came across his face.

"That's it!" Brayden exclaimed. "The trash basket! It's in the trash basket!"

The boys ran into their cabin and went straight for the trash basket. Sitting on the beds besides the trash were Jordan and Jeff with stop watches. As Jason grabbed the blue treasure box from the basket, Jordon stopped the timer.

"That's 1 hour 32 minutes for the Blue Team!"

"The Buff Team box is still here," Matthew said. "That means we won!"

"Not so fast, boys," Jeff said. "Buff started five minutes after you. If they're not back before my timer hits 1 hour 37 minutes and 1 second, you're the winner."

As much as the boys wanted to open their treasure box, they wanted to win more. The four boys sat on the bed with their eyes glued to Jeff's timer. When the clock got to 1 hour 35 minutes, they started their countdown.

"1 hour 35 minutes, 1 hour 36 minutes, 1 hour 37 minutes …. 1 hour 37 minutes and 5 seconds!"

SLAM! The porch door swung wide and closed as the Buff Team boys ran in and went straight for the trash can.

"We won!" the Blue Team shouted.

"We beat you by 5 seconds!" Jason bragged.

"Big deal," Jake said. "Buff is still gonna win Color War and the Song Fest."

"Boys!" Jeff snapped. "Did you already forget about good sportsmanship?"

The boys looked from one to the other, smiled, and ran to the unopened treasure boxes. As they tore into them, out came candy of all kinds—Kit Kat bars, Snickers, chocolate kisses, gummy bears, licorice sticks, Nestles Crunch, Milk Duds, and Hershey's bars. All talk of who would win or lose Color War and Song Fest had been forgotten. As they unwrapped the candy and began to chew each bite of their new-found treasure, they knew they were all winners on this last day of Color War competition.

That night, Song Fest took place. Just like at Camp Mineola, the boys at Adiwando were well prepared to perform their cheers, fight songs, and Alma Maters. When the judges announced the scores, the Buff Team was the big winner. Not only did they beat Blue in Color War, but they had aced Song Fest, too. Although the Blue Team campers were disappointed, they were not going to let it get the best of them. They had been at Camp Adiwando long enough to know that sometimes you win, and sometimes you lose. The thing that was more important was how you played the game.

Brayden

Dear Mom and Dad,

Color War is over. Jason and I were on the Blue Team. We lost, but that's okay cuz it was so much fun. It ended with a Treasure Hunt. The prize was a big box of candy—so many candy bars! Don't worry. I didn't get sick and even brushed my teeth.

Two days to go, and then we come home! Can we go to Jaxson's straight from the airport? My mouth is watering just thinking about a triple scoop ice cream cone. Can't wait!

Love,
Brayden

Jason

Dear Mom and Dad,

This is it! My final letter! In a couple days, your favorite son (ha, ha!) will be home. I know you can't wait.

Me neither. I love camp, but all our pals back home are waiting for the return of the Hoffman boys. The neighborhood is not the same without us!

So, start the countdown. See you at the airport!

Love,
Jason

16.

48 Hours to Go!

Back at Camp Mineola, everyone was getting ready for the final banquet. This was the best dinner of the summer! So, the girls spent the afternoon washing and blow drying their hair and putting on make-up. Make-up was really not allowed, but Director Fran never said anything if the older girls wore eye shadow, blush, or lipstick on this very special night. She even looked the other way when girls in Intermediate Camp, like Rebecca and her friends, wore make-up, too.

After the girls finished with their blush and lip gloss, they put on white dresses, which they had saved all summer for this very special night. When the bugle blew for dinner, the campers left their cabins and walked slowly to the Dining Hall. They wanted to make sure they looked perfect when they arrived for the banquet. Reaching the Dining Hall, they couldn't believe how different it looked when they opened the doors. Passing through the doorway, campers saw lots of black and white balloons floating above them. Tables were covered with sparkling white cloths and had beautiful black and white derby hats as centerpieces.

As they walked towards their seats, they were greeted by the Senior Flats camper waitresses. They were wearing black and white derby hats just like the ones on each table. Each waitress was serving mini egg rolls with duck sauce and pigs in a blanket with mustard or ketchup. The girls could not grab the food fast enough.

Once seated, the feast really began. There was a crisp green salad and then juicy steak topped with mushrooms and loads of French fried onion rings. Dessert was best of all—Chef Billy's famous chocolate fudge cake!

When the dishes were cleared away, no food was left on any plate. Directors Neil and Fran stood up to get the girls' attention. With microphone in hand, Neil began to speak.

"Before we begin our special end-of-year program, the very first thing we need to do is thank Chef Billy and his amazing staff for all the wonderful food they prepared for tonight. Come on out of the kitchen and take a bow."

As Billy and his staff walked out, the campers and counselors stood up and began to applaud, cheer, and stomp their feet. Everyone liked the kitchen staff, who worked so hard cooking their favorite meals all summer long. They especially loved Billy, who had been the camp chef for over 40 years. He knew all the girls well and was just like a grandpa to them. When the applause and cheering finally ended, Billy and his staff left, and the program continued.

"This has been one of our best summers yet at Camp Mineola," Neil said. "I want everyone here to stand up and give yourselves a round of applause. This summer was the greatest because of you!"

Everyone jumped up. Once again, cheering, applause, and the sounds of stomping feet echoed throughout the Dining Hall. Then Neil put up his arm for silence.

"It is our tradition to have a few girls from our oldest cabin—Senior Flats—speak about their summer at Mineola. When we hear their words, you will understand why Fran and I believe that no camp can compare to ours."

Three girls came forward. Although all of them gave great speeches, none was as good as the last one. It was a letter written by Sophie. She had been Blair's camp sister all summer long and had made sure that she never felt homesick again.

Dear Camp Mineola,

Goodbye! After 8 amazing summers, my days as a camper are over. I can't believe it has gone so fast! When we leave here the day after tomorrow, I will be crying like so many of us do when summer is done. But my tears will not be tears of sadness. I have nothing to be sad about. I have had so many incredible summers here, and I'm a better person because of it. When I came here at the age of 8, I was shy, afraid, and had a hard time making friends. I was so, so homesick. But thanks to Neil, Fran, and all my wonderful counselors, I learned how to make friends, become confident, and even independent. Learning how to be on your own far away from home and solve problems is a big thing. Camp Mineola has helped me to do all that. And the most important thing is that I have made friendships for a lifetime!

So, when we leave here in 2 days, I will take with me amazing memories and wonderful friends. I also hope that Fran and Neil will welcome me back in a few years to become a Camp Mineola counselor. And maybe I will become the kind of caring counselor I was so lucky to have for the past 8 years. Thank you, Camp Mineola, for helping me become the happy and confident person I am today!

Love,
Sophie

All the campers stood up and started cheering for Sophie. When all her friends in Senior Flats ran up to give her a hug, Blair, her younger camp sister, was first in line. She knew exactly how Sophie had felt long ago. Blair was so thankful that Sophie, Directors Neil and Fran, her counselors, and her new friends in Buttercup Burrow had been there for her all summer long. Not only was she no longer homesick, but she couldn't wait to come back again next summer.

The girls left the dining room cabin by cabin and walked slowly back to their bunks. With one more day to go, they had a lot of talking to do before they said their final goodbyes.

17.

24 HOURS TO GO!

It was the last day of the summer. The boys at Camp Adiwando were packing up their duffle bags and getting ready for their final dinner and campfire. When the bugle blew, all the boys ran to the Dining Hall. Just like at Camp Mineola, dinner on the last night of camp at Adiwando was always the best. A giant buffet of all the campers' favorite foods greeted them. There were chicken nuggets, chicken wings, pizza, tacos, and even hamburgers and hotdogs from the outdoor grill. The best part was dessert. Just like the first night of camp, a huge ice cream bar was set up with all kinds of toppings, including hot fudge, whipped cream, butterscotch sauce, marshmallows, and sprinkles.

Stuffed to the max, the boys exited the Dining Hall to assemble one final time at the bonfire. Like their weekly tribal council, *Tree of Value* awards were given. But the one award that all the boys were waiting to hear about was the one for "All Around Camper." This award was always given to one of the boys on the Mainland's Senior Row.

"Who do you think is gonna win?" asked Jake.

"I don't know," said Ethan. "But it's gotta be one of us seniors."

"Shh!" whispered Brayden.

"Okay, campers," said Buddy. "We're down to our last award for the summer. Every week, we have recognized so many of you for showing enthusiasm, loyalty, sportsmanship, friendship, achievement, or cooperation. Your names have been posted on our *Tree of Values*, and we are so proud of all of you! But our *All- Around Camper* Award is different because it is given to one Senior Row camper who we feel has shown all six of these values all summer long. It is always so hard making this choice because we have so many deserving campers. After a lot of thought, your counselors and I have decided.

"The camper we have selected is actually here for his first year. It is unusual to give this award to someone who is new to Adiwando and our *Tree of Values*. But this young man—Oliver Wells from London, England—learned about our six values quickly...."

All the kids in Senior Row immediately stood up and began to cheer for Ollie. Raising his hand, Buddy signaled the boys to sit down so he could continue speaking.

"When Oliver arrived here, he had to make a whole new set of friends. He had to learn games not played in London and adapt to the American way of doing things. This was not easy, especially on the day of his very first baseball game, when he didn't know which way to run around the bases. But Oliver figured out baseball and every other new sport he learned. Most important, he worked hard practicing Adiwando's six important values. Oliver is always enthusiastic; cooperates with counselors as well as campers; shows good sportsmanship in all competition; knows how to make friends and be loyal to them; and has shown great

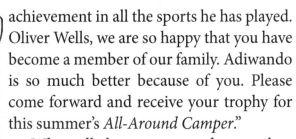

achievement in all the sports he has played. Oliver Wells, we are so happy that you have become a member of our family. Adiwando is so much better because of you. Please come forward and receive your trophy for this summer's *All-Around Camper.*"

When all the campers and counselors stood up and started cheering, "Ollie! Ollie! Ollie!" Director Bud joined in, too. As much as all the Senior Row campers secretly wished they had won the award, they knew that Ollie truly deserved it more.

After getting his trophy, Ollie joined his friends. When they all finished congratulating him and giving him high-fives, the bonfire was lit. As the flames got higher and higher, they began to crackle. Buddy picked up his golden branch and called up all the boys from Cabins 25-28.

"Do you boys remember passing this golden branch from our *Tree of Values* to each other at the beginning of this summer?"

"Yes!" they shouted in unison.

"What job did I give you at that time? Do you remember?"

"Yes!" shouted Ollie. "We needed to prove ourselves worthy of *the Tree of Values* if we wanted to graduate to Adiwando's Island Camp next summer."

"Right, Ollie," said Buddy. "You certainly have done that, and so have all our Senior Row campers standing here. Congratulations, boys! All of you are now officially welcomed to Adiwando's Island camp next summer."

"And as for the rest of you, who will be moving up to higher cabins on the Mainland, we look forward to seeing you back here, too. As the flames of our bonfire burn brightly, I want you all to take a mental picture of this very special moment and remember this...."

Buddy paused for a second and then continued. "You will leave Adiwando tomorrow morning, but Adiwando will never leave you. Its image will be burned forever in your soul!"

All the campers stood up and started cheering.

"Adiwando! Adiwando! Go, Adiwando!"

Then the Senior Row campers, who were still standing with Buddy, took the lead. The Buff Team boys sang their Song Fest Alma Mater, and then the Blue Team sang theirs. Since these special songs spoke so beautifully about campers' love for Adiwando, it was the very best way to close their last bonfire ceremony. As the fire began to slow, the boys knew it was time to call it a night. Walking slowly back to their cabins, Brayden and Jason glanced across the lake.

"Look, Brayden!" Jason shouted. "Mineola has a bonfire, too!" I can't believe we can actually see the flames burning from here. That's really cool!"

With smiles on their faces, Brayden and Jason returned to Bunk 28 for one last night of fun before they had to say goodbye to their Adiwando friends.

18.

Homeward Bound!

Campers at Mineola and Adiwando were up at the crack of dawn. The travelers had a long day ahead of them, especially the kids from far away states and countries. After bus rides to Boston, many campers would be boarding planes to go home.

At Mineola, most of the girls had been up all night saying their final goodbyes to all their friends. Between lots of hugs and tears, they were writing bus and plane notes to each of their bunkmates. This was their final chance to share one last message with each of their pals, which could be read over and over again all school year long.

At Adiwando, the last night was more about playing pranks on each other, cracking jokes, and eating whatever was left of the campers' secret stashes of candy. After many reminders from their counselors to settle down, the boys fell asleep.

Neither the girls at Mineola nor the boys at Adiwando were happy when Reveille awakened them at 6:00 AM. They all rolled out of bed, dressed slowly, and stuffed their remaining belongings in their duffles and backpacks.

Breakfast this last morning was a quick buffet at both camps. But most campers were not really hungry so early in the morning. As they waited in line to grab donuts and bagels to take with them on their buses, the first departure announcement was made.

"Will all campers going to Boston Logan airport report to Bus 1."

"That's us!" shouted Brayden. "Come on, Jason, we gotta go. Get Dylan and Jake."

When Bus 1 was ready to go, Jason rolled down the window and yelled to his Northeast pals—Ethan, Matthew, Aaron, and Conner.

"Adios, amigos!" Jason yelled. "But don't worry. We'll be back next summer to wallop you on the basketball court."

Before his friends could answer back, the bus revved its engine and took off.

Back at Mineola, the bus to Boston Logan airport was ready to load. Unlike the boys, the girls were not so eager to respond to Director Neil's boarding call. As the girls walked slowly to their buses, they could not stop from crying and giving final hugs to their friends. With gentle prodding from their counselors, the girls got settled on the bus. Maddie didn't really mind saying goodbye because her two newest friends—Blair from California and Abby from Texas—were going to the airport, too.

As the bus went down the gravel path and then through the Mineola wooden arches, the girls took one last look  at the sun rising over Lake Winnipesaukee. It was going to be another beautiful but very quiet day at Camp Mineola for girls.

19.

LANDED!

At 4:00 PM, the Florida campers landed at Fort Lauder-dale-Hollywood International Airport. As the plane pulled into the gate, their thoughts were no longer about Camps Adiwando and Mineola. All they could think about now was seeing their parents and going home.

"Mom! Dad!" Rebecca and Maddie shouted.

"There's our girls!" Dr. Hoffman said, beaming.

While the girls hugged their parents, Brayden and Jason came running off the jetway.

"Out of the way!" Jason shouted, as the boys moved in for hugs.

"We missed you so much!" Mom exclaimed.

"Can we please go to Jaxson's before we go home?" Brayden asked.

"Please, please, please," the girls begged.

"Absolutely. Ice cream it is!" shouted Dr. Hoffman. "Get your backpacks and let's roll!"

Thirty minutes later, the Hoffman family was seated at Jaxson's ice cream parlor on benches at a long, wooden table munching from a big bowl of warm popcorn and looking at menus.

Just as everyone had finally made up their minds about what they would order, a waiter dressed in a red and white stripe shirt, apron, and hat came to the table. In his hands was the biggest ice cream sundae you could ever imagine, with sparklers blazing on top. An old-fashioned fire siren was blaring throughout the restaurant announcing the *Kitchen Sink Sundae* that had made the restaurant famous.

Inside a huge bowl were six of the biggest scoops of ice cream topped with hot fudge, strawberry sauce, marshmallows, whipped cream, sprinkles, bananas, and cherries.

"We ordered everyone's favorite flavors," Mrs. Hoffman said. "Chocolate, vanilla, cookie dough, mint chip, coffee chip, and coconut."

"What are you waiting for?" Doctor Hoffman asked. "Dig in!"

With the burned-out sparklers removed and spoons in hand, the six Hoffmans began to eat and didn't stop until the entire bowl was empty. None of them could believe they had eaten the whole thing!

Dr. and Mrs. Hoffman looked at each other and smiled. Their favorite foursome was finally home. Although they had been away for a long time, they knew that Brayden, Rebecca, Jason, and Maddie would always remember the last seven weeks as *the best summer ever!*

Thank You Notes

෯ First, I want to thank my four children—Benjamin Wander, Robin Sherman, Joshua Wander, and Mollie Wander. The three books of my *Triple Trouble Plus One* series would never have been written if it weren't for them! Although these novels are works of fiction, the personalities of the Hoffman foursome are based on my own triplets plus one more when they were children.

෯ *Sleepaway Camp—The Hoffman's Best Summer Ever!* is based on the sleepaway camps where both my children and I went for so many summers in our youth.

- Thank you, Bart Sobel, owner and director of Camp Winaukee in Center Harbor, NH, for inviting me to camp to talk about Winaukee's history and the amazing experiences my sons had there almost three decades ago.

- Thank you, Nat and Ann Greenfield, owners and directors of Camp Robindel in Center Harbor, NH., for speaking with me to reminisce about the wonderful times my daughters and I enjoyed at Robindel.

I am so appreciative to all of you for the information you shared—much of which has been incorporated into this novel.

❧ I am also grateful to Camp Robindel alumni campers and parents of campers who took the time to speak with me about their camp experiences. Thank you, Stacey Schweiger (Robindel parent), Nina Heller (alumni Robindel camper), and Ali Yurman (alumni Robindel camper).

❧ This book wouldn't have been written without help from students who have gone to other sleepaway camps. I was so fortunate to have a number of campers who shared their experiences. Thank you to the following:

- Lehrman Community School of Miami Beach, Florida students: Sam Goldstein, Erik Gross, Franco Roitman, Isaac Sokol, and Ryan Bienstock.

- Hochberg Preparatory of North Miami Beach, Florida students: Meyer Cusnir, Zachary Kaplan, Solomon Sion, and Isaac Tawil.

❧ I continue to be so grateful to my mentor, Ellen Brazer, published author of two novels and one non-fiction book. For each book in the *Triple Trouble Plus One* series, Ellen has been my sounding board. Each time I finished writing one of my books, she actually sat with me as I read them aloud. Her suggestions greatly enhanced each novel in this series. Thank you, Ellen, for always being there for me. Your guidance and friendship mean the world to me!

* As many times as, an author revises and edits a novel, it is never enough. Professional advice is always needed. I am fortunate that I was able to turn for the third time to Integrative Ink Editing and Publishing Services, who added the final touch with their superb editing, book design, and layout of this novel. Thank you to Editor Stephanee Killen for her time, effort, and professional expertise.

* Finally, I would like to thank my husband Stephen. You have been by my side for 40 years quietly encouraging me to fulfill every one of my dreams. Being an author of children's books has been one of those dreams. I am so appreciative of your always being there throughout my writing process. On those painful "writer block" days, having your support and encouragement meant so much! I look forward to many more decades together with you, our children, and our grandchildren. Who knows? Maybe someday, the newest generation will be Robindel and Winaukee campers!

ABOUT THE ILLUSTRATOR

Carlos Alvarez Cotera is a Cuban born artist who lives and works in Gastonia, North Carolina. His passion for art began with drawing when he was a very young child. As a professional artist for the past 18 years, he has experimented with all kinds of materials, including pencil, watercolor, acrylic, oil, clay, glass, tiles, and even jewelry making! Mr. Cotera spends most of his time with painting. According to him, *"Art is what I was born to do."* Not only does he create amazing works of art, but he also loves to teach students. Carlos Alvarez Cortera says, *"It is a privilege to teach others and help them improve their abilities and see what has become second nature to me."*

CPSIA information can be obtained
at www.ICGtesting.com
Printed in the USA
BVHW081142270819
556811BV00001B/166/P